D1245235

# JIGGS

BY

# DENNIS CAPOFERRI

This is a work of fiction. Names, characters, places, and incidents either are the product of the author's imagination or are used fictitiously, and any resemblance to any persons, living or dead, business establishments, events, or locales is entirely coincidental.

JIGGS Copyright © 2018 by Dennis Capoferri
All rights reserved. No part of this publication may be reproduced, stored in a retrieval system, or transmitted, in any form or by any means, electronic, mechanical, photocopying, recording, or otherwise, without the express written permission of the copyright owner, except in the case of brief quotations embedded in articles or reviews.
Cover design by Ali Mogar
Published by Dennis Capoferri
ISBN: 978-0-692-04145-1

*For Tess and Jiggs.*

*For Zach, Alex, Kyle, and Max.*

*For all who follow.*

# CHAPTERS

# PROLOGUE

She sat in the wheelchair, staring out the window of her room. Overlooking the small parking lot, it offered a good view of the street as well. Theresa was thankful for that. Some of the rooms at Pickering Manor were interior rooms, some had views of open space, of trees and lawn. But Theresa's room looked out upon the world. Life happened outside her window. Regular, everyday life. Go to work, come home, shop, eat, clean, walk. *Boy*, she thought, *they don't know how lucky they are.*

It had been seven years since a stroke put her on the wrong side of that window. Seven years, but her hope never wavered. *When I go home, first thing I'm going to do is make a big pot of sauce, then chicken soup, spinach and rice, vegetable soup...*

She loved to cook but more than that, she loved to give. As soon as she finished making any of her signature dishes, containers were filled, phone calls were made and most of her production went out the door. Always accompanied by her signature, empty threat... *bring my container back or you won't get any more!* It was never just about cooking. It was always about giving.

It had been forty years since she lost her husband. Fifty-two years old when it happened, she never entertained the thought of finding someone new. She'd had her marriage. It lasted twenty-six years. It was all she ever wanted, her dream come true. You don't replace a thing like that.

Theresa met Jiggs in 1946, when she was twenty-six, married him in 1947. They had a son in 1949 and a daughter in 1955. On a house hunting trip one day in 1953, Theresa fell in love with a small bungalow in Morrisville, Pennsylvania. They lived and raised their children there until 1973, when Theresa's life without Jiggs would begin. She would spend many more years without him than with him. Good years, happy years, but those twenty-six years shone so brightly, no matter how far she journeyed from them, she could always look back and see their glow.

Theresa talked about Jiggs all the time. Her memories, shared with her children, her grandchildren, her great grandchildren, her friends, gave her comfort and warmed her heart. She could still, after all these years, close her eyes and clearly see him.

On this sun-filled afternoon, she stared through that window at the world where life happened and waited for the day when she would be on the other side of that glass. Living.

# LOOK AT THAT BOX SPRING AND MATTRESS.

*Sunday, July 14, 2013. Morning.*

There it was again. That voice. That whispering voice. Words drifting in on a breeze. Snippets. Snippets of a conversation between passing strangers on a busy sidewalk. Bits of whole sentences that, if not for ambient noise, would be longer and make sense. I never seem to be able to hear enough words. Just... snippets.

I parked the van at the curb and sat there, looking up at the house. In that short, silent moment, as the engine stilled, and no new sound had yet taken its place, the voice came: *Look at that box spring and mattress.*

Words floating on the air, entering my ears, or as I was beginning to suspect, already in my head. I thought I'd been hearing voices for a while now but couldn't seem to recall a specific, prior occurrence. And I was having trouble remembering the recent past. Yesterday. An hour ago. The short distance a person can see into the future now seems to apply to my rear view as well. No problem with old memories. That shit is crystal clear. I guess that's the way it is when you get older. Or sick.

My father died of a brain tumor when he was sixty. He was OK one day, had weakness in his hand the next and six weeks later, he was gone. That was forty years ago, and although I don't know if he heard voices, a thing like that tempts you to make a connection.

I was at the house to get mom's bed and take it to storage. Might just be my thoughts about all I had to do in the coming weeks. My thoughts speaking to me. Yeah, like that's a *thing*.

Still behind the wheel, I looked again at the house. Aside from the number of years I'd spent breathing, the longest chapter of my life was about to end. One that started in 1953 would end this day in 2013. This would be my last visit to the house on Grove Street, the house I grew up in, the only house my parents ever owned. Eight hundred square feet of cozy, cute, charming, adorable bungalow. What realtors say when what they mean is: *small.*

It was a modest house with a living /dining room or double living room if you didn't have a fancy table, an eat-in kitchen, two small bedrooms and a bathroom with a tub, but no shower.

I had one bedroom, and in 1955, when my sister came along, she got the other. Mom and dad slept on a sofa bed in the living room. Later, after I moved out in 1971, Cleta moved into my room and mom and dad took a bedroom. Finally living a normal life. But as it turned out, not for long.

The house was clad in cedar shakes, painted a reddish brown. Dad and I repainted it over the years with paint purloined from American Bridge, my father's place of employment. If there's a bridge somewhere rusting, it's probably because the paint meant for it is on the walls of 131 Grove Street.

A coal furnace dominated the basement. Giant, asbestos-wrapped ducts ran from it in all directions. On delivery day, coal would rumble down a chute, placed through a window, into the basement. With great noise and black dust, the fuel dropped into the coal bin. I would run to the basement and watch the pile grow, straining the wooden walls of the bin. Noise and dirt, a boy's little slice of heaven. Eventually, my father replaced the asbestos tentacled monster with an oil burner, one fourth the size and one tenth the drama.

I pictured my other favorite space: the attic. A centered walkway, made of one-by-twelves, three wide, ran the length of the space. At the very front was the half-moon gable vent, press-fit in place. It was easy to pry out. The porch roof was below it and I would climb out for a bird's eye view of the neighborhood and, often, my mother standing on the sidewalk, wondering where I was, looking and calling up and down the street for me to come home.

Walking up the driveway, I could see the sagging, dirt-floored garage. Hard to believe that thing is still standing. Hang in there, garage. You only need to last one more week.

I unlocked the stained walnut, atrium style front door and stepped into the living room. The house was nearly empty now. Only mom's bed remained. Everything else was either sold or in storage. That's where I was taking the bed... to the storage unit.

After several trips moving things with my van, here I was again at 131 to grab the bed. It just wouldn't fit in the truck on the last trip when I had help. This trip, I was alone. Eh, no problem...

drag the mattress and box spring out, leave them at the curb for trash, take the frame apart, load it in the van and done.

I thought about what the voice had said: *Look at that box spring and mattress.* Maybe it was my mind playing out what the neighbors would say when they saw that tired, old bedding leaning against the maple tree by the sidewalk.

*Alright, snap out of it*, I told myself, *you have a lot to do today.* Get the bed loaded and go. Despite attempting to focus, as I passed through the rooms, I couldn't help but see, in my mind, the tangled, corded phone in the dining room, the magazine rack in the corner of the living room, the holy water font in the hall, the hamper in the bathroom, and the breadbox in the kitchen.

In the hall, doors topped with frosted glass led to the only bathroom as well as the two bedrooms. The door to mom's room was oddly closed. I assumed the realtor, during a visit with the buyer, closed it. Nevertheless, I hesitated, listening and looking for motion through the frosted glass door.

Hearing and seeing nothing, I ventured ahead to open the door. Squeaks of metal against metal and the rattling of loose glass filled the hall. And yet with all that, it didn't disturb the sleeping figure I saw curled up, back to me, lightly snoring, on the bare mattress of mom's bed.

My heart raced. Who was this guy? Clearly it was a man, judging by his clothes and neatly cut, salt and pepper hair. Was he homeless? Even though his back was turned to me, I rejected that notion. I could tell he was wearing clean, pressed, dark brown slacks, a white dress shirt, brown belt and brown socks. His shoes were lined up neatly by the side of the bed. Brown oxfords. Hanging on one bedpost, a tan tweed sport coat and over that, a tan, wool fedora with a black band.

Oh, good, I thought... a hallucination to go with the voice. But this looked pretty damn real. Not like any hallucination I remember from the sixties. No, this guy was real.

I braced myself near the doorway, ready to act in some decisive way, like screaming or fainting or losing bladder control. I opened my mouth to shout but my voice sounded like the door I had just opened. "Hey!" I peeped. I cleared my throat... "Hey!" I shouted, "Wake up! Who the hell *ARE YOU?* And what are you doing in my house?"

The man stopped snoring and stirred. He began to roll over.

As he did, his eyes opened. So, did mine. Wide open. *Really* wide open. The pounding in my chest was strong, I could hear the beats in my ears and feel them in my neck. I backed myself against the wall sharply, slamming my head. It made the door rattle and stunned me momentarily. I reeled from the impact.

"Your house?" the man said. "Your house?" he repeated a bit louder and with more indignation. "Who the hell are *YOU*? And what are *YOU* doing in *MY* house?"

He stared at me, unmoving and seemed to be growing angrier. I was visibly shaking and seeing my fear, he realized he had the upper hand. He calmed himself with a big sigh but through his teeth said, "I'll ask you again: Who are you and what are you doing in my house?"

I took several deep breaths, trying to steady myself. I couldn't believe what I was seeing. I knew this man. Jesus Christ, I knew this man. I mustered all my courage and softly said, "Dad?"

# LOOKS LIKE YOU GOT YOUR WISH.

*Sunday, July 14, 2013. Late morning.*

His eyes searched the room. Scanning clockwise, they stopped where each piece of furniture had once been, at each of the naked windows, at the open door to the empty closet, down at the bare mattress he was lying on. Cocking his head, his eyes looked beyond me to the hall as if he might see the rest of the house. Finally, his gaze settled on me.

I was still shaking, pressed against the wall, trying to disappear into it. Seeing my father, who died forty years ago, should be a hallucination but it sure doesn't feel like one. I often imagined having him back. Just for a day, an hour. To show him my world. My family. My achievements. So he could see I had grown up, become responsible, that I took care of people, looked out for them as he had done from the age of fourteen. I turned out ok, dammit, and I wanted him to know it.

More than that, after all these forty years, I needed to hear it from him. A boy's desire for his father's approval lingers. Even at sixty-four, I still crave it. I had just turned twenty-four when he died and can truthfully say I've thought about him every day since. Sometimes with sadness, sometimes with joy, always wishing I could have him back.

He should have lived longer. He should have known his grandchildren. His great grandchildren. I didn't have grandfathers. I wanted my children to have him. Forty years' worth of wishing and dreaming...

*Looks like you got your wish,* a voice whispered.

*Did I,* I wondered? Am I losing my mind? Is it possible to want something so strongly that it simply comes true?

As scared and confused as I was at first, I found myself feeling at home with it all. I had played out this fantasy so many times in my dreams, in my moments alone. Driving. Working. Walking. Eating.

If you're a dreamer, if you dream of, say, winning the lottery, imagine what you would do, leaving out no detail, like a *true* dreamer, then when you *do* win the lottery, you simply put your dream into action. No hysterics, no crazy whooping and running down the street screaming. You were ready for this.

Planners prepare for the ordinary. Dreamers prepare for the incredible.

I realized I *was* prepared. And even if it's due to illness, physical *or* mental, my father came back just as I always dreamed...

He was staring at me now. Not rattled at all. Puzzled maybe, but totally in control. After what seemed like hours, he spoke... as though reading from a list.

"Who are you?" "Why are you here?" "Where is my family?" "Why is my house empty?"

He was sitting at the edge of the bed. His feet reached for his shoes and once inside, he crouched to tie them, all the while keeping eye contact with me. Shoes tied, he stood and took a step towards me, waiting for me to answer his questions.

"I'm... Dennis. I'm your son. Dennis," I stammered.

Lunging, he grabbed the neck of my shirt, twisted it and pulled me towards him. "Who *ARE YOU!*" he shouted.

*Well, this isn't going exactly the way I dreamed it.*

"Dad, Jesus, I don't know what's happening here, but *I AM* your son. I know I'm older but it's me, God dammit!"

"My son is twenty-four," he shouted, "You expect me to believe you're my son? Do I look like an idiot?" He slammed me back against the wall. Not yet fully recovered from the self-inflicted blow to the head, suffered a minute ago, this new rap to the skull shook loose a forty-year-old memory...

*****

*"Something's wrong with my grip. I couldn't squeeze the toothpaste with my left hand this morning." Dad was standing at the sink, flexing his fingers as he spoke.*

*It was December 1972. I had stopped by the Grove Street house for some reason that morning, just as he finished frying bacon and scrambling some eggs. He offered it to me and I recall accepting it without protest but can't remember if he then made more for himself. Why didn't I at least insist on sharing? Funny, the things that make a person feel lifetime guilt and shame. Add it to the list of things I've long wished I could apologize for, be forgiven for.*

"*Is it* asleep?" *I asked, stupidly chewing a strip of bacon.*

*His brow arched as he sighed. Exasperation. I earned that look often.*

"*If it was* asleep, *it would have* woken up *by now, don't you think?*"

*I'm pretty sure* don't you think *was meant as a separate sentence.*

"*Well, what do you think is wrong? Maybe a pinched nerve?*"

"*Maybe. I guess I need to see Dr. Dougherty. And your mother doesn't know yet so keep your mouth shut. I'll tell her.*"

"*I don't remember you ever seeing a doctor for anything.*"

"*Yeah, well, I guess I never needed to.*"

*Mouth full of eggs, I stared. Until then, it hadn't occurred to me that he never went to the doctor. If he got sick, he got better. I was suddenly seeing him in a different light. A light that illuminates the shadowy place where a father's mortality dwells. Hiding from the innocent, naïve gaze of adoring children. The different light switched on and just like that, I grew up.*

*He took my now empty plate, set it in the sink and rubbed his wrist again. He seemed to be wearing a different look on his face.*

*One I was unfamiliar with. He looked* vulnerable.

*Several days passed before he went to see the doc. Mom went with him and later called to say dad would be going to Helene Fuld Hospital for some tests. She sounded shaken. Mainly because in the few days between his telling me, then telling Mom and my sister, Cleta, then visiting the doctor, his left arm weakness had become much worse. In fact, his left leg was also now affected.*

*Yeah, I was twenty-four years old, married, living in my own apartment. Yeah, I had a job and a child. Yeah, I was a grown man. But he was still my father, my safe place. Heroic and strong. Men remain boys a long time in many ways. The image of the father as hero, I imagine, gently adjusts over the years as the father ages and the son matures. My adjustment was destined to be a bit more radical. He was only sixty. This shit happens to old men, doesn't it? My father's not old. He builds, he fixes, he learns, he knows, he remembers. This shouldn't be happening now. This shouldn't happen for a very long time.*

*They did a brain scan, saw nothing. Did other tests too but couldn't find anything pointing to a cause. It was, after all, 1972. The stone age when compared to modern medicine. So, they sent him home, telling him*: you probably had a mild stroke, *fitted his leg with a brace and scheduled physical therapy sessions. Thank you, tribal witch doctors.*

*Over the next few weeks, things rapidly deteriorated. One day, driving dad home from a therapy session he said, "I didn't have a stroke. Strokes don't keep getting worse. I have a brain tumor. It's just not big enough yet for them to see."*

*He knew what the doctors had yet to determine. When he went back into the hospital in early January 1973, the tumor had grown enough to be detected and its location made it obvious there was little hope of recovery.*

*He died on the 29th of January 1973. In the fucking hospital. Alone. We were there a lot in the preceding weeks, but you simply can't be there all the time. Mom was home, I was at work, Cleta was at school. Mom got the call, called me and sent my uncle to bring Cleta home. I guess all of us were alone that day until the three left standing could be alone together.*

*I think, quite often, people die when no one is looking. I've come to believe it's possible to do that. Choose to die when no one is looking. Protecting loved ones, shielding them from life's horrors to the very end. And even though the family sees the ever slowing, shallow breaths... the ones that shake but don't quite extinguish faith... and despite being in a coma, a person can choose to hide from them the final breath. The one that marks the end of life and the bludgeoning of hope.*

*That cold, cloudy day in 1973... everything changed.*

\*\*\*\*\*

My mind snapped back into focus. He still had me in a choke hold, but his grip had relaxed a bit. I pried his hand loose. "Actually, I'm *sixty-four*, not *twenty-four*. You're sixty. Or at least you were when you died in 1973. This is 2013." I was trying to control the shaking while I massaged my battered head.

His demeanor abruptly shifted. He went back to that silent, thoughtful stare. Studying me. He was considering what I just said. Not because it made sense, but because he always made considered responses to everything.

"One more time... who are you?" He re-tightened his grip and slammed me against the wall yet again.

"Would you stop that, for Christ's sake?" I yelled.

His grip relaxed again so I broke free, turned and lowered my pants.

"Remember I challenged Jerry Materacky to a fight when I was nine? I was drinking Ovaltine and believed it would make me strong like they said it would on TV? He knocked me down and I fell on a broken bottle? Look. The scar. Look at the scar!"

His face cringed. "OK," he said, "Pull your pants up! Don't do anything like that again without warning me first!"

He seemed to be considering this unusual evidence but then with his head oscillating east to west said, "That's not enough. A scar on your ass is not enough."

I reached for my wallet, "I'll show you my driver's license."

"What's that gonna prove? My son had a friend in print shop make him a fake when he was seventeen."

"Yeah, I know *I did,* but that was 1966, this is 2013."

I slid it from my wallet. A Pennsylvania Driver's License with photo, holograms, security strips and other magic. No high school print shop forger could ever hope to make one of these. My face, my date of birth, my name... proof!

As I handed it to him, my cell phone rang. I pulled the iPhone from my pocket and said, "Wait. I gotta take this."

"Take this? Take what?" he said, watching as I swiped the screen and raised the phone to my ear.

"Hey," I said, trying to sound as though nothing was wrong or odd or I hadn't just found out that everything I thought was, wasn't. I felt like Bruce Willis realizing he's dead or Charlton Heston seeing the Statue of Liberty buried in the sand or Chazz Palminteri noticing his cork board was made in Skokie, Illinois.

"What? No, no, nothing's wrong. I'm at Grove Street getting ready to take the bed apart."

"No, I'm fine. I can handle it alone. It's not heavy. I don't have to lift the whole thing *at once*. It comes *apart*."

"I'm *not* snapping at you. I'm just trying to understand something here. Something in the house. Yes. No. It's complicated. I'll explain it all to you later. Look, we both have a busy week, but we'll talk and then I'll see you Saturday, ok?"

"Ok, see you later."

"Who were you talking to?" he asked.

"Cleta. My sister... your daughter. She worries."

His eyes followed as I tapped the "END" button and placed the phone back in my pocket. Then back to the license. Then to my face. Back to the license.

While he stood there trying to process what he just saw and heard, I bolted from the room, out the front door to the porch. The tenants hadn't yet cancelled the newspaper and today's issue was by the door. I grabbed the paper and ran back to the bedroom.

"Look. Today's paper. Look at the date!" I cried, shoving the paper towards him.

He roughly took the paper from me and mumbled as he read, "Bucks County Courier Times. Sunday July 14, 2013."

He quickly flipped to other sections for confirmation. Local News, Sports, Finance. All had the same header. He saw stories that made no sense to him:

*Phillies Not Same Team That Won 2008 World Series*

*National Average Wage for 2012: $44,321.67*

*Pope John Paul II to be declared a Saint*

He flipped back and forth, "I... I don't get it. I don't get it."

Finally, lowering the paper, he looked at me. He seemed dizzy. After a couple of false starts, he slowly said, "Let me get this straight. The year is 2013... You're my son, you just talked to Cleta on... a-a walkie talkie and the Phillies won a World Series?"

"They also won in 1980 but let's try to stay focused."

He wavered, retreated to the bed, felt for it and sat, staring straight ahead. I quietly studied him. With photographs and a few 8 mm films as evidence of his countenance, I knew what he looked like, moved like. He died before camcorders so there was no voice to help paint the memory. I had forgotten the feel of his presence. I remembered his words but could no longer hear them. It all came rushing back. Like the last forty years never happened. But they did happen. And here he was, the exact same man he was before he died. Before he got sick. Sixty years old... vital, talented, astute, observant, smart, intuitive, quick. Here he was, just as I dreamed so many times. My wish. My wish granted.

He turned to look at me. "Now what?" he said.

I started to laugh. Not a *"That's funny"* kind of laugh. More of a *"Holy shit, I just drove my car off a bridge and didn't die"* kind of laugh. I mean, here I am looking at my back-from-the-afterlife father, four decades after he left. He's looking back at me, thinking it's Saturday, 1973 when it's actually Sunday, 2013.

A voice agreed, "*That's far from normal, isn't it?*"

My laughter stopped in its tracks. *It's all connected,* I thought. Him being here, the voices. It must all be part of the same thing. I have a tumor or I'm losing my mind or it's simply a distant radio. *Yeah, let's go with the last one.*

I was jolted back to the here and now when he spoke, "What am I doing here? How is this possible? I don't remember where I was. How is it that I wake up in my bedroom in 2013 and the last thing I remember, it was 1973? I can see now that it's you. Your face... It's you."

I tried denying it: "You're not real. You're dead. It's impossible. Plus, I'm hearing voices."

"Not real? Want me to slam you against the wall again?"

"No, I'm good, thank you."

He was beginning to breathe harder. Finally, with one deep breath, he calmed himself and asked, "Why is the house empty? And where is your mother? Is she...?"

"No, she's still with us. She had a stroke in '06. She's in a nursing home. I had two daughters with Ellen: Amy, who you knew briefly, and Dana. We got divorced, I married Donna. She had a daughter, Tracey. Mom moved in with me and Donna in '92. In Levittown. We've been renting this house since but now we need to sell it to cover the cost of nursing. That's why it's empty," I explained.

"Donna died two and a half years ago, Cleta's married, lives in Royersford and I have four grandsons. *You* have four great grandsons."

"Four great grandsons," he said, repeating my words.

He raised his head to look at me. "How old are they? The boys. How old?"

"Amy's oldest, Zach and Alex are twins... they're 14. Kyle is Tracey's, he's 13. Max is Amy's, he's 13."

He continued to look at me, processing what I just said. "You're the first in four generations to know your grandchildren. Your great grandfathers saw their children leave Italy for America, never to see them again, let alone their grandchildren. I never knew my grandfathers. You never knew your grandfathers. I didn't last long enough to really *be* a grandfather. But finally, you get to be one."

"Well, I'll tell you something," I said, "I was convinced that wasn't going to happen. Like there was some sort of family curse. When Amy was pregnant with the twins, I thought about that a lot. I had crazy nightmares like one where a big bag of cash fell from a passing plane and landed at my feet. Then, when I bent over to scoop up the cash, a second bag fell on my head and killed me."

He stared at me with what looked like a mix of amusement, bewilderment and sadness. "I'm sorry your wife died. What happened?"

"She had cancer. Her passing was peaceful and pain free." After two years, I'm still not used to people expressing sympathy. Never know quite what to say. I always wind up saying things to comfort *them*.

"And your mother had a stroke? Just like her mother, huh? I'm sad to hear that," he said in a low voice.

After mom's stroke, her savings dried up quickly, paying for nursing care. The rent we collected couldn't keep up, so we turned to Medicaid for relief. Medicaid requires that all assets be "liquidated" and the resulting cash "spent down" until you're so close to broke you can almost taste the cat food. We were liquidating 131 Grove Street.

"This is all so much to take in. What do we do now? Do I live here now? In 2013? Do I live out another twenty or thirty years and die again? What the hell do I do now?"

"Well, we can't stay here. We have an offer on the house and I accepted it. So, let's load the bed and leave. No matter what the solution is to the bigger issue, it begins with taking this bed and leaving here. OK? One step at a time."

"OK, but not just yet," he said. Grabbing his sport coat and fedora, he abruptly got up and walked out of the room.

"Wait, where the hell are you going?"

# Man, old people
## hate to throw out anything.

*Sunday, July 14, 2013. Early afternoon.*

I followed him as he raced down the hall, opening closets, looking in the bathroom, the back bedroom. He threw open the attic door, started up, then retreated. Out to the dining room, the kitchen...

"Dad," I said, "We have to go. The buyers might be stopping by. They wanted to measure some rooms and I don't know how I'm going to explain you."

"What do you mean, explain me? Say I'm your cousin or something," he replied, clearly distracted by his inspection of the kitchen cabinets, his handiwork.

"Well, ok, but nobody dresses like you're dressed. Maybe I could say you're just off the boat."

"What's wrong with how I'm dressed?" he asked, looking down at his clothes.

"Well, you're 40 years out of date. Wait, I think you were out of date then too. Oxfords and a fedora? And look at those pants. Those pleats. You look like you're wearing an accordion. Let's get to my house and you can wear some of my clothes. We're about the same size. You can roll up the cuffs a turn or two, so you don't trip."

"Still have your smart mouth, I see," said my five-foot-six old man.

With that, he abruptly turned and bolted down the basement steps. I followed, having for the moment, given up trying to persuade him. It was obvious now that he wasn't ready to leave. He glanced at the pantry, then moved to the larger basement space and stopped.

"Where are my tools?"

"I have them. And some new ones I think you'll like. I even took the faucet handle from the hose bib by the chimney as a souvenir. Now can we please go?"

"A *soofineer!*" he said in broken English, mimicking the way my grandmother, his mother in law, would say the word.

He silently stood and stared for a moment, then turned and ascended the steps. He moved a bit slower that he had on the way down. He helped me disassemble the bed, then we carried the mattress and box spring to the curb. I ignored his protests that they were worth keeping.

A voice... disconnected, soft, whispery... commented: *Man, old people hate to throw out anything.* Like sound from a TV in the next room that you hear only in moments of silence... *Man, old people hate to throw out anything.*

We loaded the frame in the van quickly. I was afraid one of the remaining neighbors who had known him would see us but the street was empty. I grabbed his hat as we loaded the truck and threw it in. "Enough with the hat, James Cagney".

We got in. He reached behind the seat and retrieved his hat, put it on and crossed his arms, staring straight ahead. Smiling at this bit of petulance, I fastened my seatbelt. He watched and copied without comment and we drove off. I could see him looking back at the house. He kept looking until it was out of sight, then sat quietly with eyes closed, for several minutes.

Finally opening his eyes, he scanned the interior of the van. He looked across the dash, pausing at the iPhone I had placed in its holder and the cords connecting it to the stereo and lighter socket.

"So... what is that? A walkie talkie? A phone? That's what, a portable phone?" he asked, still staring at it. "What's the range?"

"Range? No range. You can call anywhere in the world. You don't need an operator and don't need to say *roger* either. Unless you're talking to someone named Roger, I guess, but..."

"Do me a favor," he interrupted, "Try and just answer my questions, then stop talking until I ask another one."

"Yeah, like you ever answered a question with less than 300 words."

"Ok," he said, conceding the point, "let me see it."

He took it from me and as he studied it, his fingers touched the screen, brushing the *Contacts* button. The contact list sprang into view. "What happened?" he asked.

I started to explain but didn't get very far when he said, "Oh, I get it. You touch a button to turn something on. But there's no button, just a picture of a button. You touch the screen. Damn!

How does it do that?"

Then he touched the *Home* button as if he knew what to do and the app closed.

"Holy shit! Did you just get lucky or figure that out?"

"I don't know," he said thoughtfully, "I get... messages... in my head... I guess... from the other world... telling me what to do... telling me how things work."

"Really? That's incredible!"

"Yeah. My hat is the antenna."

"Having a little fun there are ya, old man?"

"Don't be a nit wit," he said, "When there's only one real button on the thing you gotta figure it's the one you push to end things, switch things or start over. I might be dead but I'm not stupid. And don't ever touch my hat again."

I should have known. He was always good at grasping the way things worked and if there was a logic to it, he could quickly understand it. He opened different apps, closed them. "What do all these do?" he asked.

"How about for now, you play some music. Bottom right button."

"What do you mean? There are songs in this thing?"

"Yeah. Three thousand or so."

"Obviously, not records or tape" he said, exhausting the list of recording methods he was aware of.

"No, it's called a flash drive and it's smaller than a quarter. I have no idea how to explain it. For now, think of a song you want to hear. Or an artist."

He thought a bit and then asked, "How about Glenn Miller?"

"OK," I said, "Press and hold the big button until you see a microphone and then say, *Play Glenn Miller.*

 He looked at me like I was setting him up to be tricked, but I gestured *just do it* in Italian sign language.

"Play Glenn Miller", he said with exaggerated enunciation and pauses between each word, like the way he would, when I was a boy, explaining the obvious to me at those times when it managed to elude me, which was pretty often.

Siri announced, *Playing Glenn Miller Orchestra. Shuffled.*

*In the Mood* came from the van's speakers. I turned the volume up and saw him close his eyes as a thin smile acknowledged the triggering of a happy memory. "Play Louis Prima," he shouted with an enthusiasm that had totally replaced the skepticism he showed earlier.

The music started, and he just shook his head in awe of this magical device. "What's the name of this thing? What's it called?" he asked.

"It's called an iPhone or a Smart Phone," I said. "Everybody has one. They store music, pictures, guide you as you drive, access the internet..."

"Internet? What the hell is internet?"

"*The* internet. Later, Dad. Here, check this out while you listen. I brought up the mic and told him, "Say, *Take me home.*"

The map appeared, and the voice navigation started. His jaw dropped. Unable to move his eyes from the screen, he spoke: "I'm gonna be really pissed if you tell me this came out in 1974."

I laughed, "No, it's not that old but it's been around a while."

"Does it triangulate somehow? It must. How else can it know your position? But it has to keep doing it over and over almost instantly. This is incredible! How's it work?"

"There's a bunch of satellites that orbit the earth as fast as the earth turns so they're always in the same place relative to us. The phone calculates how far you are from each satellite and..."

"It triangulates your position!"

He watched the screen a while, transfixed by its movement, detail and accuracy. Finally, he took a break from his screen scrutiny. "So, you're a painter?" he asked, motioning towards the rear of the van where shelves holding my tools and supplies lined both sides.

"Uh huh. It wasn't exactly my plan but it's how things turned out."

He nodded, "You don't have to tell me how *that* happens."

"Yeah," I laughed, "I guess not. I'll tell you the details later. Right now, I'm busy being amazed at how comfortable I am with all this."

"All what?"

"You. Being here. I mean, my day started out like any other and quickly turned into a trip to the Twilight Zone. I should be screaming or crying or in a straightjacket. Instead, I'm showing my father from the 70's my iPhone and catching him up on all the family news. *'Oh, hi dad! Back from the dead are ya? Nice to see ya! Look at this cool phone they have now!'* I feel like I died and went to heaven."

A voice, from nowhere and everywhere... *first heaven.* If smoke could speak, this is how it would sound... *first heaven*

"You're ignoring your own advice. You said to take things one step at a time."

"You're right, I'll stop. I only want to say that I think I'm accepting this as natural simply because I've imagined it and played it out so many times over the years. Now that it's *actually* happened, it seems right and normal."

"I suppose I get that," he replied, then added, "But it's far from normal. Make no mistake about that."

I looked over at him, wearing his vintage clothes, 3-point seat belt and holding my iPhone and thought, *Oh yeah... far from normal.*

*Far from normal,* a voice agreed.

"Well, if it's so far from normal, as you say, why do you seem so comfortable with it too?" I asked.

Jiggs shrugged. "What do you want me to do? Scream? Tremble?" he replied. "It's not like I'm staring at a fire-breathing monster. I woke up in my own bed, in my own house, only it's 2013, not 1973. I'm not in any danger. It's a mystery and a shock but my family is fine, all things considered. There are people, roads, cars, stores. The only difference is, forty years have passed. Oh, and I died and came back," he laughed, "Not really all that hard to take. And we'll figure out the mystery, I'm sure."

We rode in silence the rest of the way to the storage unit. Once there, we unloaded the bed frame and he spent some time looking at the dresser and chest of drawers that completed the set. He opened a few of the drawers and stared into them, as if remembering what they held.

He rummaged around through the stacks of boxes, asking only for his sax. I assured him I had it at home. As he opened a box labeled *Jiggs,* a voice whispered, *I wonder who Jiggs is.*

Dad held up the old Westclox alarm clock he found there and said, "Why don't you use this? It still works, I bet."

"You saw the iPhone, right? Do ya think there might be a better alarm clock by now too?"

"You need something to make noise when it's time to get up.

This thing does that" he said, still holding it up, "What more do you need?"

I started to answer, then surrendered and took it from him. "Let's go, it's getting late."

He grudgingly stopped digging, we locked up and left for my house. He was silent most of the way, watching the GPS map and listening to the music.

# Heart attacks hurt, don't they?

*Sunday, July 14, 2013. Late afternoon/evening.*

I bought my house in Levittown, Pa. in 1974, a year and a half after dad died. It's the only house I've ever owned but it's been through so many incarnations, it's like I've owned several houses... all at the same address.

It was 960 square feet of nothing-has-been-cleaned-or-updated-since-1953-except-for-this-cheesy-paneling-that-is-mysteriously-sticky. A tract house that cost me $24,000.

Now, in 2013, it measures 2,500 square feet and it's sold. I listed it, had three showings and by day seven, accepted an offer. I wasn't expecting the process to go so quickly. I have less than four weeks to make a few agreed upon changes and repairs, then find another place, pack, and move to my new house... on the day I leave this one. And deal with selling the Grove Street house at the same time. The pressure was taking its toll. I wasn't sleeping well and felt like *chaos* was the new *order*.

We parked in the street. I was exhausted, maybe he was too. Do back from the grave people even *get* tired? Or hungry? I decided I didn't care just now. I was worn out and wanted to get inside, out of the public eye, where I could let my guard down. He was staring at the house, but I couldn't gauge his reaction. I saw that he took note of the "Sold" sign. His stoic expression gave no hint what he was thinking.

"Are those your cars?" he asked, nodding towards the driveway.

"Yeah."

"You have a van and two cars for just you?"

"Well, I need a van for work. And the cars; I prefer two old luxury cars rather than one new, sensible one."

"You're just like your grandfather."

"I know. I've heard the story. A race horse instead of a plow horse."

"Yep. But I like them. What are they?"

"An '03 Jaguar and a '95 Mercedes"

"I wonder what happened to my '68 Ford Galaxie?"

"It's probably a toaster and a couple of fava bean cans. Come on. Let's go in," I said.

I unlocked the front door and keyed in my code on the alarm panel.

"You have a burglar alarm? Afraid someone will steal the family jewels?"

"Not the jewels, dad. Salvatore."

"Salvatore?"

I pointed to the cage in the Big Room. Sal, my eighteen-year-old African Grey parrot, stared back. He was resting quietly on his swing, on one foot. He had been sleeping.

Dad smiled. "Hello Salvatore," he said, approaching the cage.

"Don't put your finger in. He'll bite you. He bites everyone *but* me all the time and me sometimes."

Sal interrupted. "Hello," he said, climbing down to his big perch. He never speaks to strangers. Never. He doesn't trust anyone new and if he talks at all to a new person it's to say, *Bye, see you later*, as they leave. That's the kind of stranger he likes... one that's leaving.

*That's far from normal,* a voice observed.

Salvatore lowered his head, "Scratch, please." Dad softly scratched Sal's head.

*Yeah, I didn't just see that,* I thought.

"Dad, come in here. Let's talk," I said.

He stopped scratching Sal, walked to the table and sat across from me.

"Got any coffee?"

I made a pot. He came over and looked at the Cuisinart coffee maker, reading the labels on all the buttons. "Wow. What happened to percolators?"

On his way to the table he stopped and stared at the LCD TV hanging on a swivel bracket in the space between the eating area and kitchen. He swung it back and forth... "Is this a TV?" He turned it to one side, noting its profile. "It's only an inch and a half thick!" he cried out, "and weighs... nothing! Where's the knobs?"

I slid the remote over. "Here," I said, "No more knobs."

He studied the remote a bit, saw the power button and turned it on, then I turned it off. "Not now, please. We should eat... and talk."

I produced a bottle of Sambuca and poured the coffee, setting out cream and sugar. I forgot if he used sugar. Or if he used cream when he added Sambuca to his coffee. Or if he used it at all. How did I forget that? He used neither, adding the 'buca to the black coffee.

"Want something to eat?" I asked. Looking in the fridge, I found some provolone, pepperoni, soprasetta, prosciutto, 'gab-a-goul', blue cheese stuffed green olives, cured black olives, roasted hot peppers, a jar of anchovies and a few Yuengling Lagers. On the counter was a bottle of Montepulciano d'Abruzzo and a day-old Calabrese baguette. I laid it all out on the table.

"How's that?" I asked.

"This'll do!" he mumbled through a mouthful of olives.

The 'buca laced coffee finished, I opened and handed him a beer.

He took a few slow swigs from the bottle, closing his eyes as he did, savoring the taste, saying hello to a long-lost friend. For a guy who thinks 1973 was yesterday, he somehow seemed to know he had gone a long time without a cold one.

Watching him savor that beer, I realized how much we take

for granted. How in the course of our daily lives, when we're so caught up in the bull shit that governs us, the things we have awarded false importance, we completely miss all the small and simple joys along the way. I guess that's the point of the *Stop and Smell the Roses* saying to which I might have paid more attention had roses been hoagies.

I handed him another Yuengling.

"You want something else?"

"No, I've had enough. I'm full. Maybe more coffee," he said as he pushed back from the table. I noticed his eyes shopping what remained of the food, betraying his declaration of fullness. He popped a wedge of provolone, draped with a slice of a roasted long-hot into his mouth, then he leaned back and waved his hands, "OK, now I'm done."

"Keep eating like that and this time, you can die of a heart attack," I said.

*Heart attacks hurt, don't they?* A voice mused.

"Yeah, I suppose they do," I replied.

"What?"

"Wasn't talking to you. Answering the voice in my head."

I began to clear the table. He looked at me, unsure if I was joking. Finally, he spoke. "So, does this sort of thing happen now? People coming back from the dead?"

"What?" I said, "I know things have changed but... are you kidding?"

"Well, *I* came back," he blurted out, "So, no, I'm *not* kidding."

"Alright, alright, I get your point. No, this is, I guess, a miracle. If this has happened before, I'm not aware of it. I mean, there's stories about people *dying*, seeing a bright light or their Uncle Edgar milking a cow saying, *pull up a stool, we been waitin' for ya!* Then the CPR does its thing and they come back but it's like a few minutes later, not forty years later for Christ's sake."

"Ok," he said, "So forget whether it happened before or if it's a miracle... forget all that. I don't remember anything about the past forty years. Where was I all that time? I remember getting sick. They thought I had a stroke, but it was a brain tumor. I think I came home for a few weeks, then went back in the hospital but it's a blur after that. It was January, right?"

"Yeah, it was. You died January 29th, 1973. The tumor kept growing, they operated, but you never woke up. Sorry."

"No need to be sorry," he shrugged, "Everybody dies. I think if there's anything to fear about dying, it's that you didn't do everything you could to make it easier for the ones you leave behind to get along without you."

"Yeah," I said, "I remember once, a couple years before you died, you were changing the jets on the oil burner and you gave me a quick course on how to maintain it. I thought about it later and realized why you were doing that."

"Uh huh," he replied, "I remember doing that. I remember showing you other things too. A man starts thinking that way, or at least he should, as he ages. You really need to face the fact that your days are running out and you better tell someone how things work. The things that you always took care of yourself. And be sure to tell someone where the suitcase full of cash is."

"You had a suitcase full of cash?" I asked, choking on my Sambuca.

"What? I forgot to tell you? It was under the... in the... damn, I forget where I put it."

"Really?"

"No."

"Oh."

"So, how was the funeral? Lots of people come?"

"Lots of people? The line at the viewing stretched for blocks. It took 4 hours for everyone to pass through."

"Really?"

"No."

"Oh."

\*\*\*\*\*

*January 29, 1973...*

*"Dennis, we have to decide," Mom sobbed.*

*We were in the basement of the funeral home, being shown caskets and getting an education on concrete vaults. Seems the casket goes into a concrete liner to keep the ground from sinking over time. Some cemeteries require it. Maybe most people were aware of that but I was new to it all.*

*"This one's nice, mom. I like the steely, silver color, don't you?"*

*We agreed on the silver one. It was several cuts above a pine* box but a notch or two below the faux gold plated, bejeweled model. It was dignified. Respect has a lot to do with what a family spends on a casket, but guilt may be a bigger factor. I think funeral homes know that.

"So, tell me again, what's the deal with the concrete box?" I asked the director.

"Vault, sir. There are three models. Now, the basic one is a simple grave liner..."

"We'll take that one."

Florist, priest, organist, soloist, wardrobe. A trip to the State Store for booze and Ben's Deli for food. Not much different from a wedding. A ceremony followed by a party.

The viewing is held the night before the funeral. The immediate family arrives first and views the body privately. It's not an easy moment. It's when the finality of it all hits you over the head like a hard-learned lesson. Seeing your loved one dressed for a night on the town like some kind of cruel joke. No more nights, no more town. We stand there and look until it all sinks in. No more nights, no more town.

Next day, casket closed, we proceed to the church, then the

*cemetery, then back to the house. Food, drink, eventual laughter, vows of love and friendship, words of encouragement. But the hardest part of this journey, you travel alone. The part after everyone leaves. The part where you realize your remaining arm has a lot of learning to do.*

\*\*\*\*\*

"Dennis? You with me?" Jiggs asked, snapping his fingers.

"Yeah, yeah... Umm, what was I saying? Right, the funeral. Yeah, the family was there, friends... the usual."

Well, there was *one* exception...

\*\*\*\*\*

*Leo could always be found roaming Bridge Street in Morrisville. He would be considered homeless today but back then he was just Leo who slept behind the Sunoco station or Ben's Deli. I don't know how Leo survived but I knew him from when I was a boy up until dad died. After that, I don't know what became of him.*

*Once, when I had just learned to drive, he flagged me down and asked me for a lift to Trenton. To a bar where you could get a glass of wine, "This big!" He used his hands to show me the size. "For only a quarter!"*

*It was 7:30 AM.*

*From when I was little, anytime I encountered Leo, he would tell me how my father had saved his life in World War Two. My father assured me, he had never met Leo before moving to Morrisville in the 50's.*

*At the viewing, just before it was to end, the door opened and Leo staggered in. He worked his wobbly way to the casket and stood there for a moment like a sailor on deck in high seas. Steadying himself, he snapped to attention and saluted. When he turned to leave, I saw the tears.*

*Leo left without saying a word. I never saw him again.*

\*\*\*\*\*

Jiggs seemed lost in thought, staring at the table. Suddenly he looked up, "Hey! Where am I buried?"

I laughed, "There's a question you don't hear every day. In Yardley, the Catholic cemetery on River Road."

\*\*\*\*\*

*At the cemetery, we gathered around the casket. The priest was saying generic niceties, giving the impression he knew dad personally. It was all straight from the playbook so my mind drifted away, turned inward, muting his words, muting the sobbing.*

*I noticed a hearse enter the cemetery accompanied by a lone limousine. The mini procession stopped near the entrance, about fifty yards away. The hearse driver stepped out, opened the rear door of his vehicle and stood by, hands folded, his breath steaming while he waited.*

*After a pause, the driver of the limo opened its rear door and a young couple stepped out. Holding hands, they approached the rear of the hearse, disappearing from my view. They appeared shortly, carrying a tiny white casket. Two handles. One for mom. One for dad.*

*From the moment dad died, I waited, wondering when I was*

*going to cry. Maybe, I thought, it was only delayed due to a need to*

*plan, to arrange. The phone calls, the gathering family, the viewing,*

*the church service... through all of it, nothing.*

*But then I saw those two handles. One for mom. One for dad...*

\*\*\*\*\*

"So I wonder, what's the point? Why am I here and why do I have a forty year gap in my memory? I can't be here just because you wished for it."

"Why not?" I replied, "It's as good an explanation as anything. You looking for logic in all this?"

"No, I don't buy it," he said, shaking his head, "I'm not here granting a wish that, I'm sure, many people have."

"Well, I suppose. If it were that easy to get your dad back, it would be all the rage. It would have its own Facebook page, there would be T shirts and a reality show."

"Huh?" replied the puzzled time traveler. But he was only half listening, he'd drifted away with thoughts unknown to me. "Dad! Gene! Jiggs! G-G!", I shouted, using all his titles and snapping my fingers, "Hello. Where'd *you* go?"

He jolted back, took a deep breath. "Hel-lo?" he asked, "You say something?"

"What were you thinking about just now?"

"I don't know. I was remembering things, all sorts of things. Little things, big things. Getting drafted, getting married, driving to the shore, painting Mr. D's house when I was on strike. All my memories at once."

*****

*"So, I yelled: Frank, wake up! I fell asleep, we're in the middle of a corn field!"*

*Mrs. D could tell a story. And she had some good ones. This was one where she and her husband were driving back from the shore. It was late at night and Mr. D was asleep in the passenger seat of their Corvair. We were all laughing hysterically. There was no end to their antics and there was no couple ever, in the history of the world, more suited for each other than Mr. and Mrs. D. Two people full of love and joy, living the happiest life anyone could imagine. Sunshine and smiles, those two.*

*We were back at the house after the funeral. Fresh from the cemetery. The food and drink began to appear but the mood was somber. Low conversation hummed in the background as the women set about readying the meal. The men opened beer, poured shots but kept respectfully quiet.*

*Until Mr. and Mrs. D appeared. They entered the house with all the subtlety of Rip Taylor. And after hugs and soft words to the immediates, proceeded to bring everyone to a happier place. A place where you remember with smiles more than tears. Where the missing one would want you to be.*

*****

"Are you tired? Do you get tired? I mean, you get hungry and eat," I reasoned, "Do you need sleep too? I know you were sleeping when I found you but maybe that's just how you're... transported. Ya know, from the other world. You're placed in some kind of suspended animation or something that resembles sleep. You weren't really asleep when I found you, just coming out of transport mode. Maybe you don't need regular sleep. Wadda you think?"

"I think you watch too many movies."

"You're right," I said, frustrated, "Let's just stick with the original question: Are you tired?"

"No."

He seemed to be thinking, about to speak, but still forming what he was to say. I waited for it.

Finally, he looked up, "I want to see your mother. I mean, I want to see your sister too, naturally. I want to see my granddaughters and great grandsons of course, but first, I want to see my wife."

How about this," I said, "The girls are coming on Saturday to take things I have no room for in my next house. Cleta and Mom too. The boys can empty the shed, maybe run a yard sale out front."

"So," I suggested, "How about we wait until everyone is here and tell them all at once? Of course, then we have to try and keep it a secret because if it gets out, the attention will be unrelenting."

He considered what I said, finally replying, "I don't know, I think it will be seen as a joke. It's too incredible for people to take seriously."

"That's not how the world is now," I said, "I don't want my daughters and grandsons subjected to that kind of scrutiny followed by the ridicule once everyone decides the story belongs in the same category as alien abductions."

"Ya know," I said, "I always felt cheated not having you another twenty-five or thirty years. I should have known you longer. You should have known me as an adult. I should have had access to all you know, all your experiences, during the years when I was mature enough to realize its value and make sure I learned all there was to know. Instead, when you died and although I was married, had a baby, had an apartment, a job, I was immature and naïve, not realizing that what I took for granted could be gone in an instant."

"For 40 years now, I've regretted my inability to see that coming. It's where my wish was born and raised. But now I'm not so sure. What I want is not important. Protecting my family *is*. If you're here to satisfy my forty-year wish but at the expense of my family's peace, then maybe you should go back."

He was looking straight at me. "Not that I have any idea how to do it but you would have me go back? Finally having what you always wanted and you would let it go?"

"You know what they say: *Be careful what you wish for.* Revealing you would turn their world upside down," I said with resignation, "I won't do that."

"What did you mean, you felt cheated not having me longer? It's not like you were a kid."

"I know I wasn't a kid but the son and father, over the years, trade roles. The father teaches, the son learns and grows and becomes the strong one. The father, in small ways, reinforces the son's confidence that he is capable, mature, responsible. The father steps back. More and more decisions are the purview of the son. Eventually, the son becomes the father, the father becomes the son. That process is destroyed when the father is taken away too soon."

I quickly added, "I mean, I did ok. I took care of things, of people. I didn't resent doing any of that. Actually, whenever I started feeling resentful or sorry for myself, I would think of what you had to do when your father died and knowing that, how the hell could I ever bitch about my life?"

He nodded, "Your grandfather wanted a farm and bought one outside of Royersford when I was 12. By the time I was 14, I had to quit school to help on the farm. Amy and Evelina quit too. Your grandmother insisted we move back to town and Sabatino give up his dream of having a farm before it cost the education of all nine of their children."

"So, he continued, "We moved back to town and your grandfather got a job at the steel foundry. Soon after, he got pneumonia and died. He was forty-two. My mother forty, I was sixteen. Amy was eighteen, Evelina seventeen, the other six kids were between two and twelve years old. I suddenly found myself sitting at the head of the dinner table with all those young mouths to feed. The way those kids looked at me, their replacement father... it scared the hell out of me."

He stared away, I suppose, seeing that table, his mother, Giovina and sister, Amy cooking and serving, the kids relying on him for everything. His head shook slowly, side to side, as, in his mind, he relived those days.

Looking back in my direction he asked, "What about my

brothers and sisters? My cousins? Your mother's side too. Who's still...?"

"Alive?" I interrupted, "Well, Amy died a year and a half after you, then Ernie, Albert, Evie, Theodore, Cleta, Oliver and two years ago Edith. Your cousins, mom's sisters, brother. All gone..."

Hearing myself saying that out loud, I suddenly felt very sad and tired. I looked over at dad. He didn't seem surprised at this news. I'm sure he expected most of his siblings, most of his generation to be gone. But I guess I didn't have to hit him over the head with it the way I did.

"Dad, I'm sorry. I guess I could have delivered that a bit more gently," I said.

He shook his head, "No, that's ok. I expected most would be gone. It's just a lot to take in so quickly. I wonder if they're wherever the hell I came from. Were we together there? Why don't I remember?"

From the other room came a few words from the so far silent, Salvatore, "I'm tired. Time for nite-nite."

"Ok, be right there, Sal."

## LIKE HE'S HAVING A SWEET DREAM.

*Sunday, July 14, 2013. Night.*

*Monday, July 15, 2013. Morning.*

I ushered Dad into the Loud Room, handed him the remote and said, "You figure it out."

I went back out to the Big Room and gave Sal his goodnight scratch. As I turned off the light, Sal quietly said, "Goodnight. See you tomorrow," then what sounded like, *Goodnight Jiggs*. I decided it was my imagination.

Meanwhile, in the Loud Room, Dad was already under the spell of modern audio/video equipment and the remote controls that operate them.

"How big is this TV? It's bigger than the one you have in the room where Salvatore is."

"It's 64 inches. The one out there and the one in my bedroom are 55's. The kitchen, workshop, office and back porch are 21's. Mom's room has a 32."

"You have eight TVs?" he laughed, "Why do you have eight TVs?"

"I dunno," I replied, sounding eight years old.

I took the remote from him and showed him how to pause live TV, watch the DVR, Apple TV and the DVD player. He removed a DVD from its case, "There's a *movie* on this?"

As I explained the finer points, he grabbed the remote from me. "Thanks, I'll take it from here. You'll keep talking till I die again."

*Sir Talks-a-lot,* a voice whispered.

He channel surfed a bit, "My God, look at that picture! It's like looking through glass at real people! I like the ratio better too, it's more natural."

He shuffled through the concert DVDs, "I never heard of any of these people. Crowded House? Three Dog Night? ELO? The Killers? Bruce Springsteen? Pink? There's someone named Pink?"

He handed me one. It was *David Byrne: Live at the Union*

*Chapel in London.* "Play this one," he ordered.

I slid it in the tray and took the remote, "Pick a song."

He studied the DVD case, then said, "Everyone closes with one of their best, so the last one, *Road to Nowhere.*"

I kept edging the volume up as the song played. He was watching intently, foot tapping out the beat.

"So, wudda think? I built the speakers, by the way," I bragged. I read somewhere that a man may legitimately brag to his father. With all others, try and use a humble brag.

He didn't answer. He seemed focused on the music and the performance. I was pleased that he was impressed with the sound but more so that he was enjoying music I liked. I don't think that ever happened during his first life.

But then I noticed a peculiar look on his face. It wasn't one that revealed his appreciation for the sound or spectacle. Something was happening. He wasn't looking at the screen anymore. His eyes were darting around the way eyes do when their owner is trying to solve a mental puzzle, to reach for an answer.

"Dad, hello, what's going on?" I asked.

He seemed to hear me but still had a distracted, intent look on his face. Finally, he said, "I don't know. I just had this feeling that I was on the verge of remembering something. I don't know what it was, but it seemed to be right in front of me. Damn, I almost had it!"

"Well, you can try again tomorrow. I'm beat. You can have mom's room. I'll find clothes for you to sleep in. The bathroom has everything you'll need."

"I'm not tired yet. I think I'm gonna watch TV a while."

He stopped the DVD and switched back to TV. I was very tired, the kind of tired that comes over you when a long period of stress ends and you finally relax. I had to force myself to stop in the bathroom and brush my teeth. I just wanted to collapse on the bed and pray for a dreamless night. I found him some sweat pants and a t-shirt, threw them on mom's bed, then crawled into mine.

I woke the next morning with my heart pounding. I had been dreaming, but as usual, I couldn't remember the details. I just knew it was troubling based on my heart rate and wet hair.

*"Like he's having a sweet dream,"* a voice mocked.

"Fuck you, voice," I mumbled, through the cobwebs.

Waiting for coherence to arrive, it struck me that maybe what transpired yesterday was a dream. A rare, remembered one. But it couldn't be. It was so vivid. No, it happened, it's real. He's asleep in mom's room.

But even if it was real, what if he's gone now? What are the rules of this game? I'm not ready for him to be gone again. What a cruel joke *that* would be. I listened, heard nothing. Finally, I got out of bed and walked the hall to mom's bedroom door. I looked in and noticed the bed was made but the pillows and sweats were missing. So, it *was* real.

I found him parked in front of the TV. "Wasn't sure you were still here," I said as I entered the room.

"I couldn't find your car keys."

"I know. I hid them. Did you sleep?" I saw that he had found the blanket I kept on the floor by the end table.

"Yeah, a little. This sofa is comfortable." Holding up the remote, he said, "This thing is amazing. I can't put it down."

Solemnly, I replied, "A man, sans remote, be no man at all."

He looked at me like I was an idiot.

"I lost count of how many channels there are. No more 3, 6

and 10, huh? And they seem to say and show a *lot* more than they used to."

He continued, "I was looking around in your workshop. Isn't that the workbench I made for Dick?"

"Yep," I replied. "So, you remember it, huh?"

"How could I forget? I built that damn thing at American Bridge. On orders from your uncle for your cousin to have at his new house. The whole time I was thinking how he never gave me any kind of break, your uncle. I guess he didn't want the other guys thinking he was playing favorites with his brother-in-law, so he went the other way and never did a goddamn thing for me. I take that back, he was very good to you. He was a good uncle to you. But God, I hated working there. Working under him. Only thing I ever had in common with him was that our wives were sisters."

I told him how when Dick and his first wife divorced, I let him store the bench in the garage at Grove Street. He never asked to have it back.

"So, it's mine now."

"Then, two years ago, when my wife, Donna died, Dick didn't

come to the funeral because his back hurt or some shit but invited me to dinner at his apartment a month later. I went there assuming he wanted to make up for not attending."

\*\*\*\*\*

*October 2011*

*I heard rustling almost as soon as I knocked. Christ, was he waiting just inside the door? How long was he there? I heard a series of dull thumps and metallic clanks as the unlocking process began. He had twenty years on me and we shared DNA. Was I destined to become as afraid of everything as he is?*

*Finally, the door opened, and I stared at my cousin. It had been almost a year since I'd seen him. He was markedly shorter, wider, grayer and balder. Liver spots on his face and arms proved crabgrass has a lot to learn. They made him look like some forgotten leftover. The kind you discover in the back of the refrigerator. The kind you throw out along with its container because knowing what it once held, how could you ever use it again?*

*I knew right away this was a mistake. Coming here. Why didn't I just keep making excuses until he stopped asking? He gave me a tour of his apartment. A walking tour when really, you could see the whole place standing still. I smiled and nodded approvingly at the grandeur of it all while I made a mental note to retain the services of a doctor trained in the Kevorkian method if I ever got this way.*

*"Want some wine?"*

*"Sure. Heroin too, if you got it."*

*He thought I was joking.*

\*\*\*\*\*

"But after dinner, he started talking politics and I realized he wanted to goad me into an argument. I don't think he ever liked me, ya know? He always seemed to greet me with the kind of smile a guy smiles when meeting his ex-girlfriend's new boyfriend. The one where, all the while you're shaking the guy's hand, you're thinking: *She left me for this asshole?*"

"I tried not to take the bait but his crude opening line

regarding the President's ethnicity caused me to abandon all hope of *that* plan working."

"What do you mean, the President's ethnicity?" dad asked.

"Oh, we have a black President. You were channel surfing all night. You didn't come across that?"

"What the hell is *channel surfing*?"

I laughed, "Did you hear me? I just said we have a black President and you ask what channel surfing is?"

He laughed too, "Yeah, right. I'm not surprised. Has a woman been president yet?"

"Not yet."

"Well, that Golda Meir is doing a good job of running Israel."

"*Did* a good job. And channel surfing is flipping around the channels on TV. So, you didn't come across any mention of the President?"

"No. I watched *Keeping up with The Kardashians, Cupcake Wars, Ancient Aliens* and *Jackass*. Hard to believe they didn't cover that."

"Oh, right. Well, he is and actually is in his second term."

"So, for the past 5 years, a black President?" he laughed,

"Dick must really be flipping his wig!"

"Oh yeah, he's out of his mind, bat-shit-livid about it. You'd think a guy in his eighties would have mellowed a bit but not him," I replied, "Anyway, he continued with more hate and anger and bigotry and the most convoluted logic you ever heard. I snapped back. Finally, my smart-ass comments are too much for him and he loses it. He sweeps everything off his coffee table, throws a mug and stands to head for his bedroom. He stops halfway there and says:

*I'll get my gun and shoot you!*

*You think I won't?*

*You're no good!*

*Your father always said you were no good!*

*You're a fucking Communist!*

*Your father told me you were a no-good Communist!*

*You think I won't shoot you?*

*You're no fucking good!*

He continued towards the bedroom. I thought, maybe I could run at him and, ya know, tip him over, but instead, I headed for the door. Since then, he moved to Florida and no one's heard from him since. Good riddance to that jerk-off."

Dad sat there wide eyed as he listened. Finally, he said, "Did you believe him? I mean, what he said, I said. Did you? Did you believe that?"

"Well, not really, but a comment like that stays in your head. It sits there waiting for you to have an insecure moment, then puffs itself up like a blowfish, seeming to be bigger than it really is. I've lived with not having a father for forty years and to have someone tell me that this father I lost so long ago, this father I wished to have back, this father I admire, brag about, tell my grandchildren about, once said that he thought I was *a no-good Communist*. Well, as insane as I know that is, it still hurts. Fuck him for saying that to me about you."

Dad smiled and said, "Well, I never said any of that. We had plenty of political arguments, you and I, but you were young and idealistic. With that long hair and hippie mentality of yours, we were bound to lock horns now and then. But *no good*? Not in a million years would I ever think or say that. You were a good person who cared for people. I was proud of you in spite of you being wrong about most things."

"Thanks... I guess."

"Sure," he said, "besides, if I did think you were no good, why would I tell him? Who the hell is he that I would confess disappointment with my son to him? What is he, eighty-four now?"

I nodded.

"Wow," he laughed, "How embarrassing would it have been to be shot to death by an eighty-four-year-old lunatic? How would you ever live that down?"

We both laughed at the mental image of a feeble, eighty-four-year-old *dick* waving a handgun, as well as the idea of finding a way to live down a humiliating death after suffering one.

"For a while I kept looking over my shoulder, ya know? I mean, he was so crazed that I was sure he intended to carry through on his threat. Once his temper kicked in, his face turned black. Literally black! Mom always said that when Dick got really mad his face would turn black. Well, it does! It's like it fills with ink. As if a squid lives in his head."

"That night," I continued, "when I went there for dinner and he answered the door, you know what he says to me? What my first cousin who I've known my entire life says to me? He says, *I want to offer my condolences to you on the loss of your wife, Donna.* I'm thinkin', *what are you, the fucking ambassador from Creepistan?* Out loud I just said, *Thanks.* Then his girlfriend appears, and he turns to her and says, *I just expressed our condolences to Denny about Donna. Yeah, aww, yeah.* She stares at us both, blankly."

Dad was listening, his jaw slack, with a look of amazement, "So you haven't seen or heard from him since then?"

"No."

"You think he's gone for good?"

"Yeah, I do."

I'd had enough of recounting unpleasant memories, "Listen, I'm hungry. Want to go to the diner? I need some breakfast."

"Sounds good. Let's go. I haven't been out for breakfast in a long time."

"I think you can leave out the *in a long-time* part or you're gonna be adding that to the end of everything you say."

He nodded. "OK."

# Turkey

*Monday, July 15, 2013. Morning.*

While he showered, I laid out some jeans, a t-shirt and sneakers. I tossed a roll of paper towels on the bed for him to stuff the shoes with. He emerged from the bedroom and reading his shirt, asked, "Who the hell is *Metallica*?"

We got in the Jag, no neighbors in sight, and drove off.

"This is 10 years old? Looks great. What's an *airbag*?" he said, reading the sun visor.

"Inside the dash and steering wheel are big nylon bags. In a crash, they inflate and save your face from kissing something hard. All cars have them now. Front ones, side ones. They..."

He cut me off, "They inflate fast enough? How?"

"They explode and instantly fill."

"Explode? What's the explosive?"

"Uhm, dynamite."

"So, you don't know."

"Right."

"What's under the hood?"

"A supercharged V8."

"Can we take it down Tyburn Road?"

"Sure."

"Can I drive?"

"No."

We took a short detour to Tyburn Road, drove recklessly fast for a while, then turned around and headed for the diner. When we arrived, I was relieved to see it wasn't busy. My head was filled with *what if we see someone* scenarios, but I kept telling myself that I could think on my feet and be ok. I was having trouble believing me.

We entered the Golden Dawn, savoring the unmistakable smell of coffee and bacon. The owner came up, shook my hand and said hello. He looked at dad, "Hello. Welcome."

OK, here we go. "Steve, this is my cousin, Gene. You can call him *Jiggs*." They shook hands and we headed to a booth.

So far, so good.

Chuckling, he said, "Seven bucks for breakfast? Is there champagne? Live music? And what the hell is *turkey bacon*?"

*Turkey,* a voice hissed... *turkey.*

"You ready to order? The waitress is coming," I asked, shaking off the voice's comment.

"Yep."

She approached, carrying a carafe of coffee and creamers, "You guys ready to order?" She looked at me, then him.

"I'll have two eggs up, scrapple, white toast and orange juice," he said, decisively.

"Same for me with grapefruit juice and rye toast."

"You got it, hon." She disappeared and reappeared almost instantly with the juice, then disappeared again.

"So, what do we do today?" he asked after downing his OJ.

I wasn't quite paying attention. I noticed my next-door neighbor had just paid his check and was about to leave when he saw me and now was heading towards us. I glanced at dad, but he had started looking through the songs in the mini jukebox.

"Hi, Dennis. Not working today?" my neighbor, Jeff asked.

"You know me," I said with a nervous smile, "Two days on, two months off."

I was getting ready to introduce my *cousin* when Jeff continued, "I wish I knew you were coming here, we could have had breakfast together. I hate eating alone. I'm sure you do too."

Dad, sitting quietly, looked at me, wide eyed. He shook his head slightly side to side and waved his finger in a *no* gesture.

"Well, I gotta go, some of us have to work. Have a good one, Den," Jeff said with a wave as he left.

We sat there staring at each other, trying to understand what just happened. We were silent right up until the waitress brought our order.

"Youse need anything else?" she asked.

Who would have imagined the first thing said by either of us after that surreal moment would be one word, spoken by both of us in unison.

*Mustard*

We ate, but only talked about some of the songs on the jukebox and how everybody seemed to be lost in their phones and the look on the waitress' face when we told her the mustard was for the scrapple. I tucked a ten under my plate and paid the check. I looked the other way while dad took a handful of mints from the bowl with the sign that read: *Take One*. Basking in the glare of the disapproving hostess, we made our way out.

Back in the car, I turned to him, "So, what... he couldn't see you? And he assumed I was eating alone? But there were two place mats, coffee cups and juice glasses. So why did he think I was eating alone? I would have assumed a companion was in the bathroom. I don't get it."

He seemed to be deep in thought. Finally, he looked at me and said, "Maybe I'm visible only to strangers. Like with the diner owner, the waitress, people like that. But anyone with a connection to you, who knows you, like your neighbor, or who knows me, can't see or hear me and any evidence of my existence, like the breakfast in front of me, becomes invisible too. Get it? Wow, I bet soon I'll know why I'm here and remember where I came from."

"Invisible is one thing," I replied, "but you're saying anything that points to your existence becomes invisible too? I dunno, sounds so complex and impossible."

"Will you listen to yourself? '*Invisible is one thing*?' Me coming back from the dead... you're ok with that, but invisible coffee cups are a bridge too far?"

I just sat there, staring at him like Randle McMurphy after the procedure. "So, all my concern about the family seeing you and their lives being thrown into turmoil was unnecessary? They won't be able to see you either? So why was the owner able to see you?"

"He only knows you as a familiar face. He might know your name, but he knows nothing about you or your family. He's a stranger in that sense and therefore can see me."

"So why can I see you?"

He shrugged, "Maybe you're the reason I'm here."

I sat for a minute trying to process what he had just said. *Maybe I was the reason?* Why? Just because I've had this long-time fantasy about him returning. What the hell, everybody has a wish, right? A deep-down desire for something beyond the pale of possibility. A passionate craving for something emotionally needed, longed for. Why would mine be satisfied? It doesn't make sense. We drove home in near silence.

*Maybe I was the reason?*

# AM I LOOKIN' AT A LONG DAY?

*Monday, July 15, 2013. Morning/afternoon.*

The ride home from the diner was quiet. Each lost in his own thoughts about what just happened and its implications. So, he's invisible to anyone close to me but visible to strangers. OK, then. I guess the list of natural laws that begins with *the sun rises in the east,* now ends with *back-from-the-gravers are selectively invisible.*

Once home, I decided to shelve losing my mind and send e-mails to everyone, reminding them about Saturday's gathering to pack, sell and loot my belongings. Dad wandered into the office and asked what I was doing. I gave him a brief explanation.

"So, you hit *send* and it's there?"

"Yeah. On their computer, on their phone. Every device is connected to every other device in the world. That's what the internet is... a web of connections between all computers in the world."

"They get it instantly. Anywhere in the world." he mumbled as he started lifting me by the arm, clearly trying to take the chair.

I let him sit, showed him how the mouse worked and then had him click the link for the Google home page.

"Type in your address," I told him.

"I don't know it," he said, "Oh, you mean before I died?" He typed it in.

"Funny. Now click on *Street View*." He did and sighed, "Are you kidding?"

I showed him how to navigate. He was hooked. He cruised all over Morrisville, then jumped to center city Philly.

He typed in his hometown address on 5th Avenue in Royersford, roamed around the town a while, then John Fitch Way in Trenton to see the ballpark that superseded his place of servitude, American Bridge. "I read your poster," he explained.

I reminded him that he could search for anything through Google.

"What should I search for?" he wondered.

"Well," I said, "Try *Watergate* so you can see how you did in your final voting *At Bat.*"

"Oh? Well, it must be bad, or you wouldn't have suggested it," he replied, giving me an arched eyebrow, "So, that poster where I read about the ballpark replacing American Bridge. What's the deal with that?"

"There was a contest in '06 to honor Ben Franklin's 300th birthday. Submit a 300-word autobiography and twenty of them would be made into big posters and displayed on bus shelters in center city. Mine was one of the twenty. Twenty out of over one million entries."

He gave me a look. I shrugged and said, "Alright, a few hundred entries. Still not bad, eh?"

"OK," he nodded, "Now I understand. I laughed when I read that it was 301 words long. Have a problem with rules, huh?"

"I like making them," I said.

"I think I'm gonna look up some of the things you wrote about. Things I missed in the forty years I was away. I'm starting with drywall screws."

"Good choice, then do cordless tools. They go together."

"Alright, I will. Ya know, I remember they predicted back in the 60's that TVs would one day be thin and light and could be hung on the wall like a painting. Amazing how they were right about that."

"Yeah, well," I said, "They also predicted Jet Packs."

"What? No Jet Packs?" He went back to searching and as I left the room he shouted, "What's *Safe Search*?"

"Yeah, don't worry about that."

With him busy at the computer, I decided to do some packing. Time was growing short and I wanted to be as ready as I could be for my move. I knew the date; I just didn't yet have a place to go. I grabbed some boxes and started packing books, then switched to dishes, then tools. Clearly, my usually organized mind was a bit distracted.

After a couple hours of this, I noticed that although I had filled ten boxes, there seemed to be more stuff scattered around the Big Room than before I started. This was not working. I wasn't ready to pack. When I was ready, I would know and approach the task logically.

I went down the hall to the office: "Hey, feel like taking a ride?" I asked the captivated web surfer.

His eyes slowly left the screen. I peeked over the monitor and saw that he had the Wiki page on 9/11 open. "I don't know what to say. It's unbelievable. What the hell kind of world are you living in? So many innocent lives. I'm glad the bastard is dead, that bin Laden son of a bitch."

"Yeah, the world *has* changed. In some ways, it's worse but mostly it's better. Lately, it's become popular to recall the 1950's, the *Happy Days*. Old-timers remember all the cute stuff like milkmen and evening newspapers but forget pollution and segregation. Life is ahead, stop looking back and pining for what you think was better but was only different... and probably worse."

"You done making speeches?"

"Yeah. Let's go out."

I had an estimate in the evening and half wished I didn't suggest going out. But things never go as planned, side trips and chores get shoehorned into the mix and pretty soon, the day becomes much, much longer.

*Am I lookin' at a long day?* a voice pondered.

"Yeah, I was wondering the same thing," my mumbled answer came.

It was a sunny day so, while dad was rooting in the back-bedroom closet for his sax I quickly washed the Mercedes and lowered the top. I went back in and found him wiping the sax with the polishing cloth he kept in the case. "I need some new reeds," he said.

"OK, we'll find a music store while we're out. You ready?" I asked.

We stepped out and seeing the car said, "Wow. I don't suppose I can drive?"

"Sure, if we get pulled over just tell the cop you've been dead for forty years and haven't had a chance to renew your license."

I had a list of six townhouses I was considering and before I scheduled showings, I thought I would do a drive-by to narrow the list before wasting time seeing houses I would have rejected from the street anyway.

We headed up Stony Hill Road to pass through Newtown and work our way towards Doylestown and Warrington where the six houses were. As we drove, he marveled at the developments that crowded what used to be endless farmland.

"These houses are huge! How can there be so many? Who lives in these houses? You ever paint any of these?" he asked.

"All the time."

"Why don't you own one of these?" my smirking father asked.

"Because you forgot to tell me where you hid the suitcase full of cash."

"Oh, right."

"So, this is the Newtown Bypass," he said, reading the sign, as we turned off Stony Hill, "Can we go through town?"

Driving down Washington Ave, I saw his head quickly turn to look up Lincoln Ave in the direction of the nursing home.

Looking at me, he said, "Your mother's nearby, isn't she?"

"Yes, how...?" I stuttered. I waited for him to ask if we could go and see her, but he just stared ahead and said nothing.

A few blocks later... "What happened to Goodnoe's for Christ's sake? Where are the cows?" he blurted, "There's nothing but stores and parking lots!"

I laughed, "Yeah, I guess it's a shock to see the changes all at once."

As if to remind me, a voice kept repeating *sax reed...sax reed... sax reed* over and over. We made a quick stop in Doylestown, bought three (*What? $3.99? Each?*), then wound our way to Easton Road in Warrington and stopped at a new, mega Wawa.

"Three sixty-nine a gallon and you have to pump it yourself? Where do you pay?" said my time travelling companion.

I waved my debit card at him, put it in the slot and started pumping. He got out to examine the pump and when the tank was full, shook his head and laughed at the total of fifty-four dollars.

"You hungry?" I asked, "Let's go in and grab a sandwich and something to drink."

We went inside, he saw the sign for the men's room and headed that way. It took longer than it should have for him to come out. When he did, I asked, "Everything alright?"

"Yeah, fine," he replied as he headed to the deli counter ahead of me. He asked the woman behind it, "Can I get a roast beef and swiss on a torpedo roll? With tomato, onion and mayo?"

"You have to use the touch screen, hon," she said, pointing to one of the screens.

Watching him stare at it, she asked, "Haven't you ever used one?"

"Of course," he scoffed, "I didn't just drop in here from 1973."

With one of those *ya get all kinds* smiles, she rolled her eyes and went back to what she had been doing before he interrupted her.

I watched him touching away. In little time, he had designed his sandwich, clicked *print*, then turned and smiled at me.

"Nothing to it," he said, handing me the slip and walking away. *Damn*, I thought, *he's no fun.*

While he shopped, I ordered my sandwich, then caught up with him. His arms struggled to hold potato chips, a Hershey bar, a power drink, a two pack of hard boiled eggs, a container of diced watermelon and a cheese stuffed soft pretzel.

I sighed and pointed, "Over there is salt and pepper, forks and napkins. Get lots of napkins."

We ate in the parking lot. He watched the people come and go, watched the cars, asking me about nearly every one: "What the hell is *that*?" he asked, as a giant pickup with huge wheels pulled in. The driver was gunning the engine, intimidating the car in front of him as if his giant grill was about to open and swallow the little Toyota.

"A Ford Compensator," I explained.

"A Compensator?" he repeated.

I held my thumb and forefinger an inch apart for him to see.

He stared for a second, then laughed, "The 21st century version of kicking the crippled kid's crutches."

"Yeah, but they're not *crippled kids* anymore, they're *handicapped*, they have a *handicap*," I corrected.

"Like a golfer?"

"Something like that."

I finished my lunch. His sandwich and chips a distant memory, I watched him polishing off the last of the watermelon wondering what his stomach thought when it saw that coming on top of the hard-boiled eggs that preceded it. And if it would reach a tipping point when he added the Hershey bar and cheese stuffed pretzel.

"So, what happened in the men's room?" I asked, hoping for an answer before his gastric system staged a revolt.

"What? Nothing. Whadda ya mean, *what happened?*" came his innocent reply.

"Tell me what happened."

He stared back, then started to laugh, "OK, so I go to the urinal and I'm standing there and I'm looking at the plumbing above it and I don't see a handle. To flush it. So, I'm grabbing all over the pipes... nothing."

Laughing more now, he continued, "By now, the guy next to me is watching out of the corner of his eye. I zip up and start to walk away and the damn thing flushes on its own. So, I go to the sink. No faucets. So, I figure... the urinal knew when I was done, maybe the sink knows I want to wash my hands. I stood there waiting for the water to flow but nothing happened."

"And then..." I lobbied for more.

"And then, the other guy comes to the sink next to me, puts his hands under the spout and water comes out! He turns to me and says in that slow and loud speech you use for foreigners... like if you say it slow enough and loud enough in English, they'll understand... *mo shun sen ser.*"

I was laughing so hard I could hardly utter a reply, "What did you say?"

"Grazie, signore."

While I laughed, and coughed, he said, "So I go to the paper towel dispenser, wave at it and a towel comes out! Success! Then I go to leave and I'm waving at the door for it to open when another guy comes in, sees me waving, waves back and says, *hi*."

Since I still couldn't talk, he added, "What the hell, they make a bathroom where you don't have to touch anything but when you go to leave, you have to grab the door handle all the non-hand washers grabbed."

"Yeah, I never thought of that," I said.

"And I guess they didn't either."

He had finished his bizarre meal, showed no sign of distress other than that caused by the telling of the men's room tale, so we drove off. The townhouses I wanted to see were nearby.

"You should buy the one with the finished basement. That could be your new *Loud Room*," he commented as he read the listing on my iPhone, "And it's been for sale nine months. They'll come down on the price."

"Yeah, that one is my favorite. I'll arrange to see them and hope I can settle the same day as my sale." I suddenly felt more at ease about the move.

There was a Wegmans supermarket nearby, so I suggested we stop before heading home. "You can have your own cart. A small one," I told him.

"Damn! This place is huge!" he cried as we entered the lot, "It's the size of six supermarkets."

In the vestibule, we grabbed carts, turned the corner and when he saw the interior, said, "Can I go back and get a big cart?"

"Yeah... no."

He sulked off to the left while I went right. When I found him forty minutes later, he was at the cheese counter doing some tasting. By the look on the cheesemeister's face and the exasperated clerk busy re-weighing, re-wrapping and re-labeling, I guessed he had tasted everything they had to offer.

"What the hell are you doing?" I leaned in and whispered.

"Trying a few different cheeses, what's it look like?" he shot back.

"It looks like you don't know the definition of *a few*. Did you at least take something to buy?"

He pointed to a cart that I had assumed was someone else's. He had gone back for a big one after all. On top of a mountain of *holy-shit-what-the-hell-did-you-buy,* was a snowcap of cheese.

He thanked the relieved clerk and asked, "Where can I find crackers?"

*You trying to be here all day?* a voice asked.

I shook it off, figuring that until I smelled burnt toast, I had little to worry about. I escorted Jiggs to the checkout and while he watched... with fascination... the scanning process, I watched... with fascination... the parade of food including what looked like the entire olive bar.

He gave me a sheepish look when the screen read: *$327.34-Is this amount OK?* I sighed and pressed *yes.* The receipt was as long as Isadora Duncan's scarf. We loaded the trunk, the back seat and drove off.

"How about a coffee for the ride home?" I suggested, "I think there's a few dollars left in my checking account."

We stopped at Starbucks. He studied the menu on the wall until I finally said, "Just order two coffees."

"I'll have two small coffees," he told the young barista.

"Yes sir, two talls. You want room?" the soon to be *sorry-I-took-this-job* kid asked.

"Well, first of all, I want *small* not *tall* and room to do what?"

"Room for cream and *small* is *tall.*"

"You call *small... tall*? What do you call *medium*?

"Grande."

"You call *medium* the Italian word for *large*? What do you call *large*?

"Venti."

"You call *large* the Italian word for *twenty*? Do you have *extra-large*?"

"Yes, *trenta.*"

"So *extra-large* is *thirty*. Threw in some logic there just for fun, eh?"

"Anything else, sir," said the befuddled barista, praying there wasn't.

Back in the car he said, "That place will never succeed with confusing names like that."

I just smiled.

"Had enough of the modern world for one day?"

"Oh yeah, let's go home. I'm starving."

*Jesus...*

## MAYBE YOU KNOW HIM
## FROM THE SENIOR CENTER.

*Monday, July 15, 2013. Afternoon/evening.*

When we got home, I unpacked the food with the intention of putting it all away. Jiggs, like a bulimic piranha, tore open packages, sliced cheese, unwrapped candy bars, opened pickle jars and dished ice cream. I stood back to avoid being bitten.

"Now I know what it is," I observed.

"What, what is?" he asked, spraying cracker crumbs.

"Your super power. I thought it was just *selective invisibility*. But that's nothing compared to your ability to endlessly eat."

He was busy making a chocolate sundae, "Dammit, forgot to get maraschino cherries."

While he ate, I gathered the things I needed for an appointment I had that evening at seven. It was a comprehensive interior design project and all the sub-contractors would be there. I considered taking dad but he would have to wait in the car. I wasn't going to let him come in with me, invisible or not.

So, I left him home alone and hoped that he would be satisfied watching TV, going online and listening to music. For added insurance, I pulled out boxes of old photos for him to look through. As I walked out the door, he was spreading them all over the kitchen table. *Good*, I thought, *he's busy.*

The client was north of Princeton, New Jersey. The drive alone would take an hour and a half. And there was a lot to discuss. I might be gone for 3 hours. Most times, these appointments are scheduled during the day. This was a rare evening appointment. As it turned out, no one was late and we wrapped up quickly. I pulled in the driveway at 9:15, earlier than I expected.

In the dark, my mind occupied with what dad might be up to, I didn't notice the SUV parked across the street. Climbing out of the car, I turned and opened the back-driver's side door to retrieve my notes and fan decks.

I gathered them up and stood to close the door. Suddenly, I was thrust forward, my head slamming against the car roof.

Papers flying, I fell backward to the ground and into that state of dizziness and nausea where a blow to the head puts you while your body decides whether to stay conscious or go comatose.

I felt a hand grip my throat, squeezing and holding me down. A knee pressed heavily on my chest. The shock of this sharpened my senses enough for me to clearly see the man crouching over me. He was growling at me through clenched teeth and as his left hand tightened its grip on my neck, his right hand placed the muzzle of the gun he was holding firmly against my forehead.

The snarling voice formed words made of old man breath, seasoned with a pinch of spit, "I told you I would shoot you, you no good bastard. I bet you didn't believe me. I bet you laughed at me. Well, guess what? Now, I'm gonna shoot you. Believe me now? Huh? Do you?"

Although I was scared shitless, this perennial smart-ass wanted to say, "*Oh, hi Dick.*" but his chokehold made it impossible to speak. Just as well. Those are not the words I would have chosen to be my last.

He squeezed tighter and I was once again heading towards unconsciousness. I wondered, as I faded, if he would pull the trigger before or after I passed out.

My struggle to free myself was becoming less fervent. I was getting little air and growing weaker. As blackness rapidly approached, I heard a voice, calm and low.

"Why don't you shoot *me*?" it said.

*"Hear that, pal?"* a voice joined the fight, layering its words over Dad's.

"*Great*," I thought, "*Dad can't hear the voices and Dick can't see or hear dad. And I can't breathe. This is going really well.*"

But then the old dick let go of my neck and I felt the gun no longer pressing against my forehead. His knee slid from my chest to the ground. He wheeled around, looked up and trained the gun in the direction of the voice.

"Who the fuck are you?" he barked, aiming the gun at this interloper.

I heard a voice say, *"Maybe you know him from the Senior Center."*

"You don't recognize me? Take a good look. I'll wait," Jiggs calmly replied.

Squinting, with the glare from the porch lights in his eyes, it took Dick a moment to see Dad's face in the dark. At first, nothing registered. Then, his eyes went wide and he started to shake.

"Uncle Gene? Uncle *Geeeeeen!*" he whimpered, his voice taking the tone of a frightened child.

"You want to shoot someone? Go ahead. Shoot me," Dad repeated.

"But how? How can it be? God help me!" my older cousin cried, "God help me!"

He was crying now, blubbering uncontrollably. I was afraid he might reflexively pull the trigger but had a feeling it would do no harm to my returned father. I wondered if I was right. I wondered if dad had the same feeling or simply *knew*.

Dad reached out and wrapped one hand around Dick's. With the other he took the gun by the barrel and when my quaking cousin looked up and they locked eyes, Dick relinquished his grip.

Dad took the gun, leaned down and grabbing a fistful of shirt, said, "Listen carefully, you piece of shit. Don't you ever again say that I had anything but admiration for my son. Don't you ever again threaten *anyone* with a gun. And don't you ever again show your face to any of my family. Now go."

Dick slowly got to his feet. He could barely stand; he was shaking so severely. But he forced himself to lift his head and have a final look at this apparition of his long-departed uncle.

Almost nose to nose, with clenched teeth, Dad whispered, "I said go. *Now!*"

Dick let out a tiny scream and moved as quickly as his aging legs could carry him towards his car. It took him a minute to start it, then he lurched away, narrowly missed another parked car and disappeared around the corner.

I was still on the ground, gasping for air and trying to get on my feet. Dad reached down and helped me up. We slowly made our way inside where I watched Dad put the gun in the back of a top kitchen cabinet shelf. He had to use a stool to reach it but I figured it would be bad form to make a *short joke* right after he saved my life.

I sat heavily at the kitchen table. Dad got me some water, I gulped it down and started to breathe more easily.

"Now we know why," I gasped in a hoarse and weak voice, "Now we know why."

"What are you talking about?" dad asked.

My sore throat tried to sound the words, "Why you came back. You came back to save my life. It must be why you came back."

"Alright, don't try to talk. Breathe slowly and drink the water. I'll get you some ice," he said as he walked to the fridge.

While I was bathing my bruised throat with ice chips and reflecting on what just happened, I noticed dad seemed to be lost in thought.

"*What's on your mind*?" I asked, not with words but with a shrug and nod.

"I don't think this is it. Why I came back, I mean," he said slowly, "Seems to me it would have been something, I don't know... bigger."

"Saving my life wasn't big enough?" I wondered aloud.

"Of course, that was a big thing. A heroic thing. An action taken without regard for personal safety. A selfless act. A..."

"Ok, give it a rest, Audie."

He laughed, "Look, it seems to me that once I knew why I was here, I would also know where I came from *and* where I was headed after I did whatever the hell I'm here to do. I don't know any more now than I did half an hour ago."

"But he *saw* and *heard* you. How do you explain that? Plus, how did you know he would see and hear you? You came outside and spoke to him as if you knew he would."

He thought for a moment, then shrugged, "I didn't even think about it. I just spoke and he heard. I had no idea it would work. I guess I could have looked pretty foolish, huh."

"So, I could have died with my final memory being one where my father managed to look ridiculous?"

"Yeah, you need that like you need another hole in your head."

"So maybe you're right. Maybe what happened tonight was just a side benefit of you being here. My good fortune, huh?"

"Yep, no need to thank me."

"I didn't."

"I noticed."

I sat there wondering, if saving me wasn't the reason for his return, what was? And why, when no one connected to me could see or hear him, was Dick able to? Did Dad have some ability to make himself seen and heard when necessary? When it mattered? When a life depended on it? Could he switch it on and off at will? Did he even know he could do this? Would he be able to have Mom see him?

I decided I needed to lie down so I got up from the table and headed for the Loud Room. I paused halfway there and turned back to look at him.

"Dad... thanks for, ya know," I said, fully expressing my feelings, the way men do. I felt bad that I hadn't thanked him and saying it now sounded less than heartfelt.

He stared at me, then grinned, then laughed. "What?" I asked, "Sorry, I should have said it earlier."

"No, no. That's fine. I was just wondering how long it's going to take for that .45-caliber gun barrel dent on your forehead to go away."

I reached up to feel it. Damn, it was deep. I headed for the sofa. Last thing I heard as I began to fall asleep were microwave beeps followed by popcorn pops...

# THE GUY'S OLD.

*Monday, July 15, 2013. Night.*
*Tuesday, July 16, 2013. Morning.*

I got into bed and felt like sleep would come more easily than it usually does. Maybe I need a gun to my head more often. Screw ZzzQuil. A crazy *dick* with a loaded weapon works so much better.

I dozed off quickly and dreamed. One of those odd dreams that comes right away, is vivid and you wake with a start, to find that only ten minutes have passed and you're now wide awake.

I dreamed about a simpler time. A time when a big problem was needing three pennies and having two. Facing mom with muddy dress shoes. Homework on the weekend.

I dreamed of the winter of 1959 when hope and optimism had yet to be sullied by the realities of life.

I dreamed of being ten...

*My Catholic grade school, each December, never missed a chance to raise extra funds. Students would sell boxed Christmas cards for a dollar per and received one dime commission for each box sold.*

*The nuns at Holy Trinity Catholic Grade School & House of Shame, Guilt and Torture encouraged me to go over and above what all the other kids were doing. I agreed to take two cases, holding ten boxes each of assorted Christmas cards to sell door to door.*

*Nothing to it, they said. It would go smoothly, and I would order two more cases and make even more money, they said. Great wealth awaited me, they said. Fortune was within my grasp, they said.*

*They lied.*

*First thing I noticed when I went to the auditorium to pick up my cards was how damn heavy two cases of ten boxes each of assorted Christmas cards were. I walked to school. Nine blocks. Two cases of ten boxes each of assorted Christmas cards. Nine blocks. Dammit.*

*I made it home, set out that Saturday morning with my two cases of ten boxes each of assorted Christmas cards and finding myself on Crown Street, far from home, I began to realize there were a few things I hadn't factored in:*

*1: A lot of kids sell cards.*

*2: A lot of people don't buy cards.*

*3: I have a lot to learn about supply and demand.*

*After three hours and walking twelve blocks carrying those two cases of ten boxes each of assorted Christmas cards and knocking on at least sixty doors, I had a remaining inventory of... eighteen boxes.*

*Knock, knock, knock...*

*"Hi. I'm a student at Holy Trinity and..."*

*Slam.*

*Ding dong.*

*"Hi. I'm selling Christmas cards to help lepers and crippled kids..."*

*Slam.*

*Knock, knock...*

*"Buy a box of Christmas cards! Save a Pagan baby!"*

*Slam.*

*"Hi, I'm selling Chris... Can I use your bathroom?"*

*I was beginning to think I was going to see all of Pennsylvania before I unloaded these stupid cards. It was bitter cold and oh my God, I really, really needed to go to the bathroom.*

*But I eventually sold all twenty boxes and earned two dollars. Two dollars that would not be the beginning of the financial empire I had envisioned but instead be spent making up for an even bigger blunder than the one where I ordered two cases of ten boxes each of those god-damn cards.*

*The Great Pliers Incident of 1959 happened in late December of that year, right around the time I had received those two paper dollars, the spoils of my first dalliance with Capitalism. I was in the basement, trying to crimp a piece of metal. Why? I was ten, that's why.*

*I put the thing in the jaws of my father's new pliers but couldn't squeeze them with my hands, so I reasoned that putting the pliers in the vise would increase my leverage. I cranked the handle of the vise and saw the handles of the pliers closing. But although the pliers' handles were closing, the jaws of the pliers were not. The pliers snapped into pieces. Lots of pieces.*

*I hunted all around for the pieces, found most of them, but not being skilled in welding and being sure that glue or tape wouldn't work, I was left with one alternative... confess.*

*Later, my father came home from work and settled into the corner chair in the living room.*

*"Dad?" I half whispered, after my stealth approach. He was reading the Philadelphia Evening Bulletin that he seldom lowered, once raised.*

*"Uhm, I was trying to crimp something and..."*

*The newspaper lowered, "Why?"*

*"I dunno," I shrugged, using my standard explanation for everything I did.*

*"What were you trying to crimp it with?"*

*"Your new pliers, but I couldn't squeeze them hard enough."*

*"So... Then... You..." he replied, waiting for me to fill in the blanks.*

*"I put them in the vise."*

*"Put what in the vise?"*

*"The pliers."*

*"You put something in the pliers and then the pliers in the vise."*

*"Yes."*

*"And, let me guess, you broke my pliers."*

*"Yes."*

*"Didn't you read the instructions?" he asked.*

*"What instructions? For the pliers? No. I mean, I didn't see any instructions," I replied.*

*"That's because there aren't any, but I'm pretty sure that if there were, the instructions wouldn't say feel free to put the pliers in a vise. Pliers don't come with warnings telling you not to squeeze them in vises. You know why? Because it's something you should just know. You need to learn to use tools properly."*

*His speech went on, covering many and varied topics. Once the chapter on losing an eye started, I zoned out until it all sounded like distant machinery grinding big things into little things.*

*God, I hope this ends soon.*

*"So," he said, not as I had hoped, ending soon, "Since you broke them, then you can walk to Sears in Trenton on Saturday and buy me new ones. Didn't you just earn two dollars, selling Christmas cards?"*

*So, that Saturday I walked the two miles to Sears in Trenton and bought him a new pair of pliers. They cost $1.89 including tax. With the remaining eleven cents, I bought eleven pieces of penny candy. A ten-year-old boy's version of going on a bender.*

Yeah, life was simple then, or so it seems looking back from here, from age 64. But nothing great and wonderful can be identified up close. It must be seen from another place. A place less grand, a place more complicated. You can't see sixty-four from ten, only the reverse is possible. It attracts and appeals because you have perspective, not because it was better.

If you're forty-eight and lose your job, is that a bigger problem than if you're ten and break your father's new pliers? Does a heart attack at fifty-six shape who you are more than being caught shoplifting comic books at twelve?

And yet with all the wisdom and perspective we have at sixty-four, our vision of ten is selective. We remember the good, fun parts. The bad, sad parts hide in the shadows.

But all of it, good and bad, shapes us. It all makes us who we are...

Take me, for instance. I was born in 1949. A baby boomer.

My parents decided to name me, *Dennis*. My older cousin, *Little Mary* (In Italian families, every Mary needs a qualifier), suggested it and my mother liked it. *Dennis* was the 16th most popular name in 1949. It's not the kind of name most Italian-Americans name their boys. As far as I can tell, Dennis Farina was the only other Italian-American Dennis from the 40's.

It never would have bothered me to be named *Dennis* had it not been for Hank Ketcham who, in 1951, created Dennis the Menace... that cute, little, mischievous, lovable, tow headed, cowlicked, freckle faced, overall wearing, oh-so-adorable little boy who got into all sorts of mischief and said *gee* all the time. I am not now, nor have I ever been, a person who says *gee.*

By the time I was five, the Chinese Water Torture of being referred to as *Dennis the Menace* by the endless drip, drip, drip of people who were all so proud of being the first to have thought of it, was becoming too much to bear.

Walking down Bridge Street in Morrisville, holding my father's hand, we would invariably meet someone he knew. They would shake hands, my father would turn to me, then to the soon-to-be master of wit and say, "This is my boy, Dennis."

No hand shake for me. "Well, well, well, little Dennis the Menace! Are you a menace, Dennis?" the numbskull du jour would bellow. He would laugh and laugh. My father would smile politely. I would dream of how I might inflict major suffering or a slow and painful death. I was thigh high at five. A lot of sensitive shit down there. I would imagine how, with one swift move, I could make this potato head cry for his mommy.

Between being named *Dennis* and the television character, Froggy the Magic Gremlin, I was primed to disrespect and question authority figures.

Froggy was a character on a kid's TV show in the 50's. He was a rubber doll with outstretched arms and a permanent grin. Froggy had no moving parts but if you squeezed him, he would defiantly stick out his tongue and squeak.

He would be summoned by the show's host, Andy Devine, when Andy called out, *plunk your magic twanger, Froggy!* With a *boing* and a puff of smoke, Froggy would appear on top of a grandfather clock and say, "Hiya Kids!! Hiya! Hiya!" He had a mischievous, devious, diabolical laugh but we soon came to realize that he was a friend to all kids and his reign of terror would only be visited upon adults.

Froggy was a consummate trickster. He played tricks on all adult authority figures. A guest instructor... a chef, music teacher, coach... would begin to lecture. Completely disrespectful, Froggy would utter subliminal suggestions which the instructor would robotically carry out and, in the process, make a fool of himself. Hilarity ensued and the personalities of a generation of children were being formed with the attitude necessary for the 60's to happen.

I didn't set out to be a smart ass and rejecter of all things held sacred and I suppose many people and events had a part in it, but it all began with an innocent name and a rubber frog.

I stirred from my dreamy walk down Memory Lane and felt... cold. Like I was lying on bare concrete. Cold and damp on the small of my back. My shirt was hiked up and the hard surface was drawing the heat from me. I had dull pain in my chest and abdomen. *I better turn over,* I thought, *or I'm going to have a sore back when I get up.*

*The guy's old...* a voice mocked.

Finally sitting up, I thought about the things I'd dreamed. I suddenly had an intense feeling of longing for those days. I had reminisced and remembered many times before, told the stories that made up my dream, many times before. But I never felt like this before.

I guess all the upheaval in my life... Donna's death, selling the house, moving, almost being killed by *mio cugino* and oh yeah, my father coming back from the dead... might have helped make me want my blankie.

Well, no time for that now. Better get up and work at getting ready for the move. And find something for Jiggs to do. Hmm, I do need to build those shelves...

Oh yeah, forgot to mention... A few days after buying new pliers to replace the ones I broke, two dollars mysteriously appeared in my sock drawer. Neither of us ever said a word about it.

## LOOKS LIKE THREE HOURS AGO, GIVE OR TAKE.

*Tuesday, July 16, 2013 thru Friday, July 19, 2013.*

I dragged myself to the kitchen where I found Dad already eating. He was chowing down on sunny-side-up eggs, toast and scrapple... with mustard, of course.

"I don't see mine."

"There wasn't enough."

"A pound of scrapple wasn't enough?"

He stopped chewing for a moment, shrugged and said, "Guess not."

I shook off my bewilderment at his ability to, as the Coneheads would say, *consume mass quantities,* and changed the subject.

"Dad, I was thinking... When my house was listed, the agent mistakenly included the workbench. I didn't notice it until I had accepted the offer. So, I promised the buyer that in exchange for my taking the bench, I would build a work table and shelving. Do you want to do that for me?"

He was lifting the last yolk, balanced precariously on a corner of toast. It fell to the plate as he froze, looked up and said, "You kidding?"

"Not kidding. I have to see the house in Warrington and a couple others, then the dentist and do an estimate. I thought you could design something, take the van to Home Depot, buy what you need and build it."

"Yeah, you're kidding."

"I'm not. You can take my debit card to pay. Just don't go overboard."

I told him how to get there, tossed him the keys and left. I had been so on-edge the past two days, worried about him being revealed, worried about closing on two home sales and one home purchase, that I just surrendered all concern. Fuck it. I just don't care.

I left in the convertible, not even looking back. I had things to do, things that had to be done... well, I guess I could skip the dentist.

See ya later, Jiggs. You're on your own.

*****

*Jiggs watched his son drive off. He was excited to finally have a mission, maybe not a lofty one, but one he knew how to deal with. He made a list of materials in his head while he cleared the table.*

*He wiped the counter and just as he grabbed the van keys and debit card, his eyes noticed another set of keys in a bowl, on a small table near the door. Jiggs picked them up. On the chain was one key, one of those remote locking devices and a charm in the form of a jaguar.*

*He stared a moment, shrugged and thought, "I can go to Home Depot tomorrow," as he grabbed them up. He started the car, put the gear shift in Drive and as he moved his foot from the brake to the gas, grinned widely.*

*Jiggs knew where he wanted to go and knew how to get there. Most of what had changed on Route One escaped his notice. He could only see his destination; Royersford. His hometown.*

*He started out, driving slowly. That is to say, within the speed limit, but once he reached the Turnpike and after he quickly figured out what the white box on the windshield, labeled "EZ Pass", was for, he floored it.*

*Flying past the Blue Route interchange, heading to the Valley Forge exit, not knowing about the 422 bypass, he took the ramp for Route 29. The closer he got, the more excited he felt. Driving over the bridge from Spring City, he was finally home.*

*He slowed, then stopped in front of his family home... a crooked duplex on 5th Avenue in Royersford, once crammed to the rafters on both sides with iron headed, laughing, squabbling, loving Capoferris. Each so unique and special. Each now, gone and sorely missed.*

\*\*\*\*\*

As a kid, every visit to Royersford was, for me, a treat. But especially when one of my Aunts or Uncles from out of town was also there. Cleta, Albert, Ernie and of course, my Aunt Edith.

She lived in an exotic, far away land called New Hyde Park, New York. I was reminded of this each time I would walk across the bridge from Morrisville, Pa to Trenton, NJ. On the Trenton side, just over the bridge, there was a meat packing plant. You could look down on the rear of the building as you crossed over. Parked there permanently next to stacks of animal hides, I guess used for storage, was a rusted, old truck trailer from a sister plant in New Hyde Park, NY. I would point and tell my friends that I had an Aunt who lived in that distant place, never once allowing the reality of that sight to sink in and ruin the illusion.

Aunt Edith was so very special. Soft spoken and classy, insightful and funny, beautiful and smart, sophisticated and interesting. She was to me... way before I ever used the word... cool.

Dad had 8 brothers and sisters. They lived in one half of a duplex. With only three bedrooms. In the other half, lived his aunt and uncle and their eleven children.

His dad and uncle were brothers, his mother and aunt, first-cousins. The four of them had travelled here together in 1907 from Ancarano, Italy and once here, married and settled in Royersford.

\*\*\*\*\*

*Jiggs stared at the house. Memories flooded his consciousness. He saw his mother sitting on the porch, his nineteen siblings and cousins running around the house, in and out of the doors. He laughed to himself thinking that such a small duplex with twenty-four residents, twenty of them children, must have looked more like an infestation than a habitation.*

*He put the car in gear and slowly drove off. Heading north on Fifth Avenue, he turned left on Pine and a hundred yards later found himself in front of the American-Italian Bocce Club. Jiggs was one of its founders.*

*He parked and headed to the door, then paused. What would happen? Could he enter this place as a visible man? Was it possible there were people still alive who might recognize him? And if he was visible, how would he ever get in and be served? Private club that it was.*

*He slipped in the door behind a club member who looked suspiciously familiar. "I know that guy," Jiggs thought, but couldn't quite place the old man. Didn't matter. Thanks to him, Jiggs was in full invisibility mode.*

*He made his way to the bar, taking a stool at the far end.*

*There was a plaque on the wall nearby, listing the founding, charter members. Looking at his name immortalized there, he wondered how many of the handful of Tuesday-afternoon patrons knew any of the names on that plaque. And if anyone did, how long before they were all forgotten, anonymous relics of a time long-gone.*

*Jiggs made his way back to the car and once there, felt a wave of sadness, loss and longing. He turned the key to begin the journey back to his new reality. The world he now found himself, inexplicably, a citizen of.*

*****

It had been a long day. Looking at houses, one estimate, and a trip to the dentist had me thinking, with a singular focus, about the couch. But as soon as I turned the corner, I knew a trip to the sofa wasn't in my near future. The van was in the street, but the Jaguar was gone. *Jesus H. Christ, Jiggs. What have you done?* Frustration built inside me, having no idea when he might return, where he went, or when he left.

A voice offered its opinion: "*Looks like three hours ago, give or take.*"

I didn't have long to wait for an answer. As I pulled into the two-car-wide driveway, so did Jiggs. I stared and I knew, he knew, I was staring. He busied himself looking for some non-existent thing on the floor, I guess, hoping I would get bored and go in the house. Finally, he looked over at me, grinned and waved. I shook my head, sighed, and walked to the house. I realized as I did, that the role reversal of father and son, the one we were denied when he died so young, had finally come to be.

"Where the hell did you go?" I yelled, as he entered the house.

"Guess."

"Royersford."

"Look how smart you are!"

"Do you have any idea the shit-storm you could have created?"

"I was careful. Nothing happened. You need to try and relax. Live a little."

I started to reply, then decided my original plan involving the sofa, was more important. I laid down and was asleep almost instantly. I slept until ten, moved to the bedroom, wondered where Jiggs was, decided I didn't care, and fell right to sleep again.

Wednesday morning, not taking any chances, I went with him to Home Depot. His reaction to Wegmans the other day was nothing compared to what happened when we walked through the doors of Home Depot.

"I...what...there's...how..."

"Breathe. Slowly, breathe. Easy, easy."

He finally got it together and we hit the lumber aisles, loading a large cart. Then on to hardware and tools. After hearing myself say "no" to almost everything he asked for, I realized the miracle of his presence was worth abandoning all reason and indulging all whims.

So, we left there with an air compressor, a framing nail gun, compound miter saw, router, and ten-tool lithium ion cordless kit. I only stopped him from buying tools I already had: "You got a laser level?" "Yes" "You got a cordless drill?" "Yes" "You got a chop saw?" "Yes" "You got a double-bevel compound miter saw?" "God dammit-No" So, nearly two and a half grand lighter, we wheeled it all to the van, loaded up and headed home.

He spent Wednesday and Thursday building the worktable and shelves. They were damn near furniture grade.

We spent Friday looking through old photos. Although I had seen them all many times, the stories he told that went with each of those photos were priceless. It lasted well into the evening.

"Alright, I'm ready for bed. The girls, mom, everyone is coming tomorrow. You didn't forget, did you?"

"Does that seem like a thing I might forget?"

"Right. Goodnight, then."

"Goodnight."

# Heaven is a place
# where dreams come true.

*Saturday, July 20, 2013. Morning/afternoon.*

I woke early and began sorting things that I thought would appeal to each of my daughters and my sister. Many things were Mom's and she would decide who got which of those. The things no one wanted would be held for a yard sale or donated. I had plenty for everyone to eat thanks to my personal shopper's feeding frenzy at Wegmans.

"Need any help?"

"You can go in the attic. Bring down the boxes by the trap door," I suggested.

"Are they heavy?"

"If they weren't, I would do it. You're younger than me."

"Technically, I'm 101."

He brought the boxes into the big room. "Wow," he said, taking in the sight of it all, "You sure have a lot of stuff."

He was fidgeting and wondering aimlessly around all the boxes and other things. He looked like a guy waiting to have a colonoscopy the day before his tax audit.

"I'm nervous about this," he finally said.

"I can see that. So am I. But I just keep telling myself they won't be able to see you, so there's nothing to worry about."

"I know *they* won't be able to see *me*. That's not what I'm nervous about. *I'm* going to see *them*. Get it?"

"I get it, I get it."

They would arrive at noon. Cleta was bringing mom. Amy, Tracey and Dana were coming as well as Zach, Alex, Kyle and Max... The Four Grandsons of the Apocalypse. Zach and Alex, twins, were 14. Kyle and Max were 13. Old enough to help carry, sort and move things. Young enough not to want to.

"Somebody's here," dad shouted, peering out the kitchen window.

It was Tracey and Kyle. I greeted them at the door just as Amy pulled up with Zach, Alex and Max. As they were walking to the door, Dana arrived.

They all piled in. As I talked to each of them, I repeated their names and touched their shoulder or pointed if they were too far away to touch.

"You don't need to do that. I'll figure out who is who," came dad's voice from the corner where he had positioned himself. It startled me. I held my breath, but no one heard, no one saw.

"Amazing," I uttered and hastily added, "Uh, the amount of stuff mom-mom and I accumulated. Amazing." I guided the four boys to the big room. "You guys start emptying those boxes and setting things out for everyone to see."

Kid One: "Can't we have something to eat first?"

Kid Two: "Yeah, I'm thirsty."

Kid Three: "Me too."

Kid Four: "It's unanimous."

I walked to the kitchen where the girls were chatting. "Better get some food on the table. The boys are hungry."

The three of them exchanged glances. "You want us to do it?"

"I have to supervise."

I noticed dad had positioned himself where he could watch

the activity in the big room as well as the kitchen. It looked like his head might fly off. Like he was watching a fast-forwarded tennis match on TV. He was smiling, and his eyes looked glazed.

It reminded me that I had never seen him cry. Never. The last time I thought about it was forty years ago when he died, and I wondered then, as I cried, if he had, long before, cried for his father too.

Mom told me once, the only time *she* saw him cry was when I fell from a bike, fracturing my skull and suffering a Grade Three concussion at nine years old.

*****

*June 1958*

*I don't know where my bike came from. It just showed up one day. Dad got it somewhere, somehow. It wasn't new, but it worked. I painted it red and added streamers. Then a mirror, suicide knob and an antenna stolen from an old Studebaker in the junkyard* behind Piscopo's Garage. No one asked me how I had acquired those things. No one had to.

I got good at riding it, venturing further and further from home. Even as far as Black Rock Road in Yardley where we could fly down its long, steep slope all the way to the river. Doing this "hands free" went a long way to establishing a nine-year old's street-cred.

One Friday evening, as dusk approached, we were playing a game of "Just ride towards each other really fast and try to knock the other kid off his bike". No one was getting hurt, mainly because we were all too afraid to get close enough to get hurt.

Until I did.

One well aimed kick sent me flying over the handlebars, breaking the antenna, which I thought about the entire time I was airborne, and head first into a concrete step, thirty years before bike helmets were a thing.

I became aware maybe an hour later, lying in my bed, with Dr. Dougherty, who my dad had called, looking down at me, telling my father to call for an ambulance. According to mom years later, dad was crying after being admonished by the doc for rushing to where I fell, scooping me up and carrying me home.

The ambulance took me to Helene Fuld Hospital in Trenton. The same hospital where dad would leave this world, fifteen years later. Dr. Dougherty stayed with me all night. All night. Didn't matter, they had ICU staff and neurosurgeons. He was my doctor. The kind of doctor who considered something like that his responsibility. Who wouldn't think twice about it and wouldn't bill for it.

I had a fractured skull and a Grade Three concussion. I was there for ten days, strapped down, arm tied to a board, hard-needle intravenous fed for four of them. Roomed up with a kid who had both eyes bandaged and cried incessantly. Followed by a kid who, I swear to God, chewed through the restraining net tied over his bed and ran through the corridors screeching and pummeling the nurses who tried to corral him.

I was not allowed to leave that bed the entire time. Ten days on my back, never rising, never turning. Ten goddamn days glued to the bed. Ten goddamn days on my back. I became terrified of the bedpan. I developed an irrational fear of filling such a shallow bowl and having things pile up high enough to touch me. Christ...

I was supposed to "take it easy" and have "limited activity" once I came home and I did. For a week, maybe. After that, it was *as if it never happened. Except that since then, I have never, ever*

*slept on my back. Not once. Ever.*

*****

Lunch was on the table by now, so I went to the big room to
gather the four Langoliers. As they raced to the table, which I
feared they might eat once the food was gone, the front door
opened, and Cleta poked her head in. "Hi everybody. Dana, can
you help me with grand mom?"

Dana went outside with her. I turned to look at dad, but he
wasn't there. I looked in the loud room, then the office, where I
found him.

"What are you doing? Mom and Cleta are here."

He had his back to me and when he turned, I saw he was
crying. "Give me a minute... go," he said as he waved his arm and
looked away again.

*Well,* I thought, *I'm tied with mom.*

I left him there and went out to the kitchen. Cleta and Dana
had just finished maneuvering the wheelchair through the door.

"Ready to give some things away?" I loudly asked mom.

"It's not going to rain today," she replied.

We all surrounded the table and after a minute or two, I saw dad slowly coming down the hall. He wasn't yet able to see mom. He advanced with tiny, crablike shuffles, holding himself flat against the wall. I couldn't imagine what he was going through. He was about to see the woman he had spent twenty-six years with, who had then spent another forty alone.

He finally advanced enough to see her. He started to tear-up and slump a bit but then smiled. I think he would have given anything just then to be the 101 years old he joked he was and be sitting in a wheelchair next to her.

While we ate, dad found a corner to stand and watch. The boys were well into their lunch and except for chewing and slurping sounds, were quiet. The rest of us talked about past lunches, bygone times, fun times when the girls were kids. Eventually, the talk turned to more distant years.

"Mom... how did you and dad meet?" I shouted. Even though I knew the story, I knew mom never tired of telling it. And I thought my unseen guest might like hearing it.

"Oh, you know the story. How many times are you going to make me tell it?"

"OK, if you don't want to tell it, then don't. I thought the boys might like to hear it." She loved acting as though she was being forced to tell the story she loved telling.

"It was at Bill and Glory's engagement party," she began. "I had heard some things about him and he had heard about me too. Glory's family was close to ours. Her aunt, Emma, was my best friend and Bill was daddy's cousin.

"The party was at Emma and Beanie's house. I walked into the kitchen where everyone was crowded around the table, eating and drinking. In the far corner was a stranger who I knew right away was this Jiggs I had heard so much about." As she said this, mom turned and pointed to the far corner of the kitchen, pointed and looked straight at her husband.

Dad stiffened and took a quick breath. Mom's gaze lingered and just when it seemed to me and dad that she really *was* seeing him, she turned back to the table and continued the story. "He was just standing there, his hands in his pockets and a smirk on his face." *Just the way he is right now,* I thought, erasing my duplicate smirk.

"You mean like pop-pop does?" one of the boys mumbled through a mouthful of everything.

"Exactly like that. Your pop-pop has his father's smirk. Like he's making a joke in his head or he knows something the rest of us don't."

"I know lots of things the rest of you don't."

"Here ya are, Denny," came mom's retort as she thumbed her nose.

The boys giggled.

Cleta got up and headed to the big room. "I'm going to start sorting things."

Dad walked over slowly and sat in the now empty chair next to mom. He was facing straight ahead, then slowly turned to look at her. Mom, silent now, seemed to be having a private memory. Slowly her eyes came back to the present and she turned her head in dad's direction. She stared. He froze. Finally, she turned away.

"You ok, grand mom?" Dana asked.

"I'm fine. I just had a funny feeling. Like it was a long time ago. Sometimes, in my mind, I can see your grandfather clear as day. Good thing, too. I wouldn't want to not recognize him when

I see him in heaven." She laughed with the rest of us.

A voice whispered: *heaven is a place where dreams come true.*

Cleta came back just then and added, "Sometimes I remember how I used to sit in daddy's lap, how he would bounce me and tickle me."

With that, she plopped in the chair on top of dad. He was suddenly puffed into the air like a cloud of dust, then reformed standing behind her. I gasped.

Cleta turned to me with a perturbed look, "Why'd you do that?"

"I thought you were going to break the chair."

More boy giggles.

We adjourned to the big room where the women started going through the things destined to take their places among the next generation. When does a thing become a family heirloom? When it's three generations removed? Four? Two? Is there a rule?

Some things are just *stuff.* A tower of Tupperware. A mountain of mugs. A pile of placemats. Excess copies of things I need fewer of, in my new, streamlined lifestyle. Things that not long ago, when I wasn't living here alone, when this house was alive, when Donna was alive, things that were so necessary, are now superfluous. Funny how that works.

But some things will hopefully, live on. Old photographs, Donna's crystal glassware, mom's art deco goblets, dad's tools, his lunchbox, my grandmother's pasta machine, even mom's old rolling pin. These things have meaning. They connect us to our past. Speak of where we came from. Touching or viewing these things conjures images of what life was like for the people who laid the groundwork of our existence. A vision of how our DNA manifested generations ago, before it conspired to create us. These things matter to me. I hope they will matter to the future beings that share my blueprint.

By late afternoon, my load was lightened. Everyone left. Dad watched them all leave, then silently wandered off. He appeared with his sax and headed to the loud room. He put on some music and began to play along.

I left him alone and went to my office.

# THERE ARE CRAZIER IDEAS.

*Saturday, July 20, 2013. Afternoon.*

After a while, dad came down the hall and peered into the office.

"What are you doing?" he asked.

"I have to re-work an estimate. The client wants to add some things."

"*Client*, huh... not *customer*."

"*Clients* pay more than *customers*."

"OK," he laughed, "I'll be in the loud room. Will the sax bother you? I thought I would find some music to play along with."

"Uh-uh. I'll be about an hour doing this," I said, "Hey, I just remembered something. When I was a kid, you used to play your sax in the basement but after a while, I know you felt pressure to stop from mom or even me and Cleta, especially if we had friends over or were trying to watch TV."

"How could I forget," he said, with a distinctly sardonic note.

"So, one day you were in the basement under the stairs, measuring. I asked why, and you said..."

He interrupted, "I'm going to build a soundproof room under the stairs for when I play the sax."

"Yeah, that's right." I was surprised he remembered. "And I said *you're going to play your sax in a tiny room under the stairs? And you said...*" I waved at him to finish the quote.

"No, I'll be playing anywhere I want. I'm putting the three of *you* in there."

"That was funny."

"Who says I was joking?" he shot back as he left the room.

"You know, your Fake Book is in the bookcase if you want to use it," I shouted down the hall as he left.

Fake books were song collections, illegally printed, with no royalties paid. Each song in a fake book contained the melody, basic chords and lyrics. Enough for a musician to put together a quick arrangement of any song... in other words, he could *fake it*. Most musicians had one. My father's book, spiral bound, was simply titled: *Over 1,000 Songs.*

"No thanks, I know all those songs. I'm gonna try playing along with some of your music," he shouted back.

I returned to writing my estimate and shortly heard Dean Martin singing *Ain't That a Kick in the Head,* with Jiggs on tenor sax.

I finished my work, e-mailed the revision and became aware again of the music coming from the Loud Room. After starting with something familiar, he jumped to *Joy Ride* by The Killers. I grinned at the thought of him listening and playing along to the music in my library. All he ever did, when I was young, was make fun of my taste in music and here he was passing up the standards in his Fake Book for The Killers and oh-my-God, now he's playing Pink Floyd.

I went out to the Big Room to do some packing. It was closer to the music and I was enjoying the songs and his accompaniment. The Eurythmics were finishing *Sweet Dreams* when I heard *Heading for the Light* by The Travelling Wilburys begin.

I started singing along, then stopped. I heard a sixth voice coming from the other room. It was dad. He sang as if he were reading the lyrics. I walked over to the Loud Room door and peered in. I saw, over his shoulder, the TV, displaying the album art.

Two verses and the chorus passed with Jiggs not missing a single word and when the sax solo began, he started to play along.

As the solo ended and he started to sing again, I slipped into the room, grabbed the remote and paused the song. I heard him sing, *down this same highway,* unaccompanied, then turn abruptly to look back.

"Why did you do that?" he asked, turning up his hands.

I turned up my hands, mimicking his puzzled stance, "How do you know that song? You know every word. You didn't miss a note of the solo. How is that possible?"

He was looking down now, staring at his feet. I knew he had something to say. I waited for it.

After a moment, he looked up and said, "These guys I know... George and Roy... play that song all the time. Sometimes I sit in for the sax solo."

"George and Roy?"

"Yes," he answered, walking over to the TV and pointing

at the album art, "George, and Roy." As he said each name, he touched their image on the album cover.

"They're a little hard to recognize. This isn't a photo, more like a drawing. But it's them. George and Roy," he said, touching the screen once again, "Don't know these other guys. Maybe they're still here. You know who they are?"

I opened my mouth, but nothing came out.

He snapped his fingers, "Dennis! You OK? Do you need to sit?"

"No," I said, "No. I'm not OK. Did something just happen that might lead to my being OK? No, I'm not OK. I don't know what to say."

"You can say if you know who the other three guys are."

"Sure. You blow my mind but before I get any kind of explanation, you need to know who the other guys are." Annoyed at his insistence that I answer his inane question, I regained my composure.

Moving from right to left, I pointed and said, "Tom Petty, Jeff Lynne and Bob Dylan."

"Oh, *Bob Dylan*. That uh, *Blowin' in the Wind* guy."

"Yeah, the *Blowin' in the Wind* guy. And Roy is Roy Orbison. George is George Harrison."

He stared at me.

"George Harrison, he was one of the Beatles."

"Oh yeah, The Beatles... John, Paul, George and Ringo. So that's George! How about that. And I remember Roy Orbison too. "Only the Lonely", right?"

"That's right," I said, "Now tell me what's going on before my head explodes."

He was looking down again. I could see he was getting ready to speak. I didn't know how long I could last, waiting to hear... something, anything.

Raising his head, in a low voice, he said, "I remember everything now. The song triggered it, I guess."

"You remember? Remember what... heaven? You were in heaven? There *is* such a thing as heaven?"

"It's not like that. Not like what everybody thinks. There's not a place where everyone goes when they die. Where they meet up with everyone who ever died before them."

"What do you mean? Everyone doesn't go to heaven? You mean

some go to hell? Or nowhere at all? I don't get what you mean."

"First, I'm not sure but I think *hell* is just a place they invented to keep people in line. No. I mean, there isn't one place where *everyone* goes. What would be the point of that? A place where everyone goes? An eternal reunion? With everybody you ever knew? Can you imagine how crowded it would get? All your ancestors, all the way back to the ape you came from? The introductions alone would take an eternity. *This is your great, great (times a million) grandfather, Zongak. He was the first in our family to walk erect.* There would be a trillion, billion people there, all crowded around, trying to get a spot at the railing to look over and watch all of you down on earth."

"There's a railing?"

"Look, no one is watching you, OK? We have better things to do. What... you think everyone who dies spends all their time watching those who didn't? What kind of *heaven* would that be?" And with a dismissive wave, "I lived my life, you live yours. Doesn't mean we don't miss or long for people left behind. But *moving on* means just that. It's called *the next life* for a reason. It's not a continuation of this one, just in a different place. I lived my life, you live yours."

"So, you don't watch over us? What about all the times I *felt* your presence, your support and influence? I always thought it was you watching over me, helping me."

"That's what's inside you from your time *with* me. Your memories of how I might deal with a certain issue guides you. It wasn't me looking over your shoulder after I was gone."

He continued, "Look. You live your life here. You struggle, you strive, and you have dreams. But responsibilities creep in. You sacrifice for the sake of others. Nothing wrong with it. In fact, it's admirable, noble even. But your dreams, the life you yearned-for never happens. You live with that. You tell yourself that it was worth forgoing because living a responsible life for the sake of others was much more important."

"But, you never forget your dreams. Never forget the life you imagined, and thought was ahead. Well, I don't know if it's meant to be a reward for a life *well-lived* but when you move on, one by one, you get to live the lives you might have lived here on earth."

"Lives? What do you mean, lives? You can have multiple lives?"

"Jesus Christ!" he muttered, "Look, I wanted an education. I wanted to be an engineer. Design and build great things. I dreamed of that when I was a kid. Instead, my father bought a farm and I had to quit school at fourteen to help work it. Then, after we gave up the farm and moved back to town, just as I thought I might go back to school, my father died and I had to take a factory job to support the family. I was sixteen. So, that's one dream dashed."

"In spite of all that, I managed to learn the saxophone, join a band and then an orchestra. I loved playing, making music, performing. But then World War Two imposed, I was drafted... for the duration. When I finally came home, more than three years later, it became clear that the *Big Band Era* had ended. Clyde Walton's orchestra was no more and so with no opportunity to earn a living making music, I had to get a regular job. I still had a mother, younger sisters and brothers to think of. No time to dream of making music. So, dream number two dashed as well. You see what I mean?"

I tried to process what he was saying, "Yeah, I do, I think. So, you're saying that when you moved on... to the next life or whatever it's called... you got to live out the dreams you had to let go of, while you were alive? That's what you've been doing for the past forty years?"

"Yes, sort of. But there's no *time,* as it's known here. You're in a place, doing a thing. Then, you're in another place, doing another thing. Sometimes, you're in one place doing a thing and another place playing a role in someone else's thing. No *how long,* no *when.* Nothing starts, nothing ends. It just *is.*" He stared for a moment, then touched his fingertips to his temples and did the *mind-blown* gesture.

*"There are crazier ideas,"* a voice whispered.

I shrugged off the voice. "But what about George and Roy? They made music while they were alive. It wasn't a dream for them. They lived it. Why aren't they living their dream of, I don't know, selling shoes?"

"People dream of selling shoes?"

"Just sayin'"

Jiggs shrugged, "I made music while I was alive too."

"This might sound like a stupid question," I said, prefacing my stupid question, "but did you... see God?"

"That's a really stupid question."

"Well, answer it anyway."

"Yes. All the time. He's at all the concerts and throws out the first pitch at ballgames. Doesn't always throw a strike but we pretend He did 'cuz of that *fire and brimstone* thing He does."

"Go ahead, keep screwing with me."

"I've already told you more than I should have. No one is supposed to know what comes after death. I could get in trouble for what I already spilled."

"So, you've been playing music? With George and Roy and who else?"

"Lots of others. But there are no last names. Nobody talks about their life on earth, who they were. We remember our lives. At least I did, but it's never a topic. I didn't know who George and Roy had been until you told me."

He continued, "And the faces keep changing. People come and go. From one, let's call it *heaven* for your sake. From one heaven to another. For example, I'm not going back there."

"What do you mean, you're not going back there? Where are you going? You're staying here?"

"No, I'm not staying here. This isn't going to last much longer."

My heart sank. *Not much longer?* I didn't like the sound of that. He just got here, and I have so much more to ask, to tell.

He was smiling at me, "How long did you think this would last? Nothing *lasts.*"

"Well, I had just hoped it would be longer, that's all," I mumbled, sulking like a kid with a mouthful of cotton candy, being dragged from the carnival.

"I know, that would be great." His voice took on a soothing tone.

"So, when are you leaving?"

"Soon."

"Where will you go?"

"Another... heaven," he said, making air quotes.

"You gonna tell me more?"

"Not yet, no."

I sat there pondering all he said. As strange and wonderful and bizarre as this experience has been, I'd gotten used to it quickly. I suddenly realized I was doing *exactly* the same thing I did when he was alive. Taking his existence for granted. Learning little, sharing little.

"Then I guess we better start getting to know each other."

"Yeah."

# Know what this is?

We settled down in the Loud Room with coffee and Sambuca. I let him choose the music. He turned on the Apple TV, selected Pandora and created a Big Band channel.

"So, what's it feel like to finally have your *dream* come true?" Dad asked as he put his feet up on the coffee table.

"I dunno. I feel like I need to ask you so many questions before you're gone again. So many, I don't know where to start."

We were briefly silent. I rejected trying to cover topics in any logical order. It was what had me stymied. The hell with it, just talk about whatever comes to mind. I jumped up, "I'll be right back," and left the room to retrieve something.

I came back quickly and held out my hand.

A voice whispered... *know what this is?*

"My address-book!"

"Yeah. The one you carried during the war."

I handed it to him. He started thumbing through it, grinning, reading some names out loud, others silently. He looked happy and sad, all at once.

I waited until he had looked at all the pages, then said, "Go back to the first page. The inside front cover. Read what's written there."

In pencil, in large block letters, the way he most often wrote, the way I write, was one name and address:

*Mademoiselle Denise Duboille*

*24 Rue Due Moutier 24*

*Ennery*

*(set 0) fa5 pontoise*

A small smile formed. One inspired by the recollection of a fond memory, tempered by the acceptance of it never being more than that.

"So, who was she? How did you meet her? How old was she? Tell me."

"No. Not gonna talk about that. That's my memory, I'm not sharing."

"Why not? We have this second chance to know each other and you won't talk?"

"Not about that. I don't want to share that. If I had lived and you one day, asked me about her, I still wouldn't have told you. You didn't need a second chance to ask me about that. I wasn't telling you then, I'm not telling you now."

I sat there, staring at the floor, searching my brain for another topic. One that might lead to some sort of revelation, offer insight, be of value.

"You never told me you loved me..." was what I came up with.

He was staring at me, coffee cup frozen halfway to his frozen, open mouth.

"What the hell are you talking about? I never told you I loved you? Why would I do that? What are you, a nine-year-old girl?"

"People tell their children they love them. I did. Well, maybe not as much as they do now but I did. You never did. Would have been nice, is all I'm sayin'. You never once did. How was I supposed to know you loved me?"

"You had a roof over your head. Heat. Food. Clothes. I clapped at your graduation. What more did you want? Cuddly hugs? I wanted you to become a man, not a puppy."

"So, you're telling me, you think I've become a man? That's good to hear."

"I did think that. Right up until you whined about me not telling you I loved you. Now, I'm thinking you're possibly a puppy."

We spent a few hours reminiscing, catching him up on my life and hearing about his life before me, before he was married, before the War.

He had been in an orchestra, a big band, back in the 30's and 40's. Clyde Walton and his Orchestra were quite popular on the college and ballroom circuits in the greater Philadelphia region. There were 11 musicians including my father, his cousin Funcie, Clyde the band leader and Dawn Frederick, the vocalist.

From the age of 18 until he was 30, until he was drafted, he played. It began with a small group of eight in 1930, called The Aristocrats, then blossomed into Clyde Walton and his Orchestra.

He told me a story that he claimed was an example of a typical night during his career as a musician...

*****

*The Scene:*

Sidewalk in front of the Benjamin Franklin Hotel in Center City Philadelphia.

On the marquee above the main entrance:

*The University of Pennsylvania*

*Senior Class Formal Dinner and Dance.*

Posters on either side of the entrance proclaimed:

*Music by Clyde Walton and his Orchestra*

*The Most Talked-of Band in the East*

*Featuring Dawn Frederick, Vocalist*

Inside, music echoed through the main ballroom. The

opening act, a smaller group with a male singer welcomed the crowd as they drifted in with their rendition of Count Basie's *One O'clock Jump*. This was the Senior Class event of the year. The grandest of all the dances, balls or dinners the senior class would attend. It was the event that would usher them off to a life of achievement, wealth and privilege. After all, these weren't just any college students. These were *Penn* students. Jiggs had plenty of experience with Ivy League students. They were booked for most of the Penn social events and often played Princeton University balls as well. Of course, they played Penn State, Lehigh, Temple, Rosemont, Ursinus, and more, but with all due respect to the other schools... this was Penn.

While the opening act played, Jiggs and Funcie leaned against a column along the side of the ballroom, smoking cigarettes and watching the students arrive. The boys wore tailored tuxedos, a cut above what these two observers wore to work as saxophone players in the *Most Talked-of Band in the East*. Pointing towards a poster near the side of the stage, one of many like the ones out front, Jiggs said to his cousin Funcie, "*Most Talked-of*, huh. Maybe they're talking about our cheap tuxes"

Funcie laughed, "Forget about the guys and how they're dressed, we need to concentrate on the girls."

Jiggs nodded agreement, "Look at that blonde! Oh, Mama'!"

Funcie shrugged, "Oh, what's the use, Jiggs. Those girls don't want guys like us. They're on their way to bigger things than we could ever offer them."

Jiggs shook his head in disagreement, "Let me tell you something Funce, they want bad boys, they want musicians, they want some excitement. Later, they'll marry an accounting major named *Something, the Third*. Tonight, they want some fun."

Jiggs noticed an approaching redhead. As she got closer he straightened a bit from his bad boy slouch. Keeping eye contact, with one final puff of the cigarette, he ground the butt in a nearby ashtray. She seemed to be on a course aimed at approaching and speaking to him rather than simply passing by, so he decided to say nothing and let her speak first.

She did, "Hi boys! Are you in the orchestra? With Clyde Walton?"

"I think I remember you-oo from the Fall Dinner Dance," she said to Jiggs, poking his chest as she said, *you-oo*.

"Oh, and I remember *you* too," he leaned forward to say.

"No, you don't," she giggled, "What was I wearing?"

"Now how could I answer that," Jiggs asked, "when all I could do was stare at those beautiful green eyes?"

Funcie rolled his brown ones.

Jiggs offered the giggling Penn senior his hand, she took it and he led her to the dance floor, close to the stage, where they started to dance. The opening act began to play *If you were the only girl in the world.* Jiggs sang to her as they danced. She was mesmerized.

Jiggs stopped singing and said, "I don't believe I got your name."

"Betty," came her happy reply, "That was the best! And what's your name?"

"I'm Jiggs. Happy to meet you, Betty. Listen, we're about to go on and we play till two but if you're still here, I know a place that's open all night. An after-hours place. We could dance, eat and drink. How does that sound?" Jiggs asked.

"Sounds great, Jiggs," she giggled, "See you-oo at two-oo." She poked his chest one more time.

*****

"So, what happened with Betty?" I asked.

He just grinned.

After a while, he turned and asked, "Aren't you going to the nursing home tomorrow? I'd like to go with you. I want to see what it's like there."

"Yeah, sure," I yawned, "I'm going to bed."

## One foot in each world.

*Sunday, July 21, 2013. Afternoon.*

We left the house around 1 PM for our drive to Pickering Manor. Dad had been silent most of the morning. Seemed deep in thought, lost somewhere. In the car, he occupied himself sampling music from my phone, rolling his eyes at some songs but generally, he seemed to like most of what he came across. After the "Heading for the Light" incident, he brought up the Travelling Wilburys album and checked out most of their tunes. Finally, "End of the Line" came on. He stopped sampling and let it play.

I could hear a voice speaking behind the music but couldn't understand the words. As the song ended, I heard it say... *one foot in each world.*

It occurred to me that there had been a couple of song-related turning points since he returned. I began to think another was coming soon. One I wasn't ready to accept.

We arrived at the nursing home as the song ended. Walking in, just as we were about to reach her room, he stopped me, held me by the shoulders and said, "I always loved you. I was always proud of you."

"You're leaving, aren't you," I whispered.

He nodded and squeezed my shoulders. "This is why I came back." I hugged him, not wanting to let him go but knowing I had to.

Turning the corner and entering Mom's room, we saw her near the window, writing a letter. She looked up at me and then, incredibly, at him, "I knew you were coming. What took you so long?"

She *saw* him. She *expected* him. They were both smiling as he took her hand.

"How about we blow this joint?" he softly said.

I opened my mouth to say, *talk louder,* but was cut off by mom, "I've been ready for a very long time."

He took her hand, held it in his right, and covered it with

his left. As he slowly stepped back, she leaned forward. Without effort, she rose to her feet. As she rose, the room filled with swirling light. My vision blurred from dizziness or tears. Or both.

The trappings of Pickering Manor melted away into a gauzy, white landscape populated by a young man in a tuxedo and a young woman in an evening gown. Younger than I had ever known them to be. *My God,* I thought, *this is how they began. So vibrant and vital. Handsome and beautiful. With all life has to offer ahead of them.*

They slowly danced, floating in the whiteness and light and just as the vision began to fade, they looked at me. She smiled, he winked and just like that, they vanished.

The room snapped back into focus. Just me, a bed and an empty wheelchair. I stood and stared at nothing in particular, finally turning to leave. I shoved the empty chair into the hall, tore away the tag that bore mom's name, then walked to the nurse's station and told the aide there that mom wasn't in her room and I had to leave. "Tell her I'll stop by tomorrow."

"Ok," the aide laughed. "She must be in the activity room or roaming the halls."

I figured I would deal with the *missing mom* call when it came. Right now, I needed to leave. I drove home in silence. Back in the house, I sat and re-lived the past eight days. What happens now? Soon, the nursing home would realize mom was gone. How do I handle that? And tomorrow is closing on the Grove Street house. Shit. Like I need that now.

Thinking about the past unbelievable week, I finally and deeply fell asleep, waking abruptly at 3 AM. I was shaking, sweating and out of breath. I went to the kitchen, made coffee, then sat at the computer, knowing my night's sleep was over.

While I waited for the coffee to brew, I checked my e-mail. Among a handful of the usual junk was one with the subject line: *A message to my son.* The sender's name... Jiggs. It was time stamped yesterday, 5 AM...


*Dear Dennis,*


*I hope I got it right, I'm new to e-mail and am setting this to be delivered at midnight. It should all be over by then. Since realizing why I came back, I've been trying to find a way to explain it to you.*

*You see, it's time for me to move on. To what you might call, "my next heaven", using again, my feeble attempt to explain. I've already had a music heaven, an architect heaven and others as well.*

*Your mother and I never had the time, the money or the freedom to enjoy life, to travel, to be alone with only each other, with no cares or worries. Just us together.*

*I would have wanted it to be my "first heaven" but naturally, I had to wait for her. I imagine you're feeling bowled over with all this and, of course, very sad as well. Don't be.*

*I wasn't the only one waiting for this. She was too. It's a long time, we've been apart and the past seven years for her have been more than anyone should have to bear.*

*Of course, she will miss you, miss all of you but it's her time now. I know you would all want that for her. Be happy for her. For me and her. Celebrate and remember what you had, how lucky you were to have her. No one ever gave more than your mother. Repay her with a smile and a wish for her happiness... finally living her dream. The one and only thing she ever wanted for herself.*

*I'm very proud of the entire family. The future is in good hands.*

*And I'm proud of you. Proud of your life. I know a man needs to hear that from his father. I know I left too soon for that to ever happen.*

*I'll let you in on a little secret. I spent my whole life wondering what my father might have said to me. Would he be proud? So, I wanted to be sure to tell you.*

*By the way, you're probably worried, waiting for the nursing home to call and say your mother is missing. Don't worry. It will all be as it should. I don't think I need to explain.*

*Love you, son*
*Dad*

*PS: You like puzzles? Here's one for you: East gable, west of three, east of four, south side.*

I read the e-mail twice, carefully examining each word. I was beginning to feel some degree of calm, of comfort. And an understanding of what happened and all that was good and right about it.

But what the hell was the PS about? I sat back in my desk chair, closed my eyes and thought about his words, then the coffee I brewed and had yet to drink, then the cryptic PS.

Suddenly, I had an epiphany. Heart pounding, I grabbed my flashlight, dashed to the car and drove off.

Arriving at the Grove St. house, I let myself in and headed to the attic. I negotiated the center walkway and made my way to the front gable, the east gable. I pulled my phone from my pocket and read the PS again: *You like puzzles? Here's one for you: East gable, west of three, east of four, south side.*

South was to my right. I counted three joists to the west and noticed the insulation between it and the fourth joist had a bulge in it near where the sloping roof met the outer wall. Was it always there? I don't remember it being there but why would I have ever looked.

*Don't slip through the ceiling, you close in a few hours,* I told myself as I crawled towards the ever-narrowing space and the mysterious bulge. I got as close as I could and stretched to reach under the insulation. I felt a handle and dragged the thing back to the center where I could at least kneel. It was a suitcase.

At first, I smiled, then started to laugh. This is crazy. Is it possible? I thought he was joking when he... It has to be a joke... I mean, it can't be... Right?

I slid the latch releases and they popped open. Slowly, I raised the lid.

*Son of a bitch...*

## The End

# Epilogue

*Sunday, July 14, 2013.*

Detective Quentin Burns slammed on the brakes as he parked. He hated being called out on a Sunday morning, especially *this* Sunday. His in-laws were visiting in the afternoon and he had assured his wife that he would be gracious, and more importantly, be *present*. Seeing her angry face in his rear-view mirror as he drove off, he could only imagine what was in store for him when he returned.

Despite loving his work and not being sure what he'd do to fill the time if he *didn't* work, days like this made him really want to retire. *Tomorrow,* he thought, *Tomorrow I'm turning in my papers.*

At the scene he noticed the medical examiner's wagon and only one patrol car. Good, maybe this won't take long. *Please, no foul play... throw me a softball.*

The M.E.'s assistants were sitting in the open rear of the "meat wagon". Burns nodded to Misha and Julia. Julia was showing Misha her new shoes. He was feigning interest. *At least they get overtime,* Burns thought.

There was a work van with what appeared to be parts of a bed frame inside. Burns gave it a glance as he passed, then entered the *Stow-N-Go* storage building. He saw the patrol officer about fifty feet down the hall standing outside an open unit.

"Hi Don," Detective Burns said as he shook the officer's hand, "Am I lookin' at a long day?"

"I doubt it, the M.E. thinks it's a heart attack. The woman that rents the unit across the hall found him. I let her leave. Here's her info. The guy's old and he was moving furniture alone. Look at that box spring and mattress. They must be fifty years old. Why would he save those? Carrying those probably did it. Man, old people hate to throw out anything."

"How old?" Burns asked.

"Here's his I.D. He's like 64 or something. Maybe you know him from the Senior Center."

With a sideways glance, the detective growled, "Chief owes me a favor, Don. How about a week or two in Parking Enforcement?"

Officer Don held up his hands and tried to stop smirking. Detective Burns entered as the M.E. was rising from her crouch, reading a thermometer. Burns recoiled at the sight of the thing. It was what they used to measure liver temperature and determine time of death. It reminded him of a meat thermometer and led to some disconcerting mental images every Thanksgiving, watching his wife check the turkey.

"Looks like three hours ago, give or take. And it's most likely a heart attack. Lucky you, huh?"

"Yeah," Burns replied, "Lucky me."

As many times as Burns had witnessed the routine examination of a body, he had not hardened to it. He felt a certain sadness and pity for the dead. Here this man was, lying on a bare concrete floor, his shirt hiked-up so the M.E. could stab into him with a fucking meat thermometer... all necessary, but damn; how humiliating.

"Can't you pull his shirt down? Christ, don't let him lie there like that," Burns begged the M.E.

She complied with a roll of her eyes and as Burns watched,

he noticed something odd. "He looks like he's smiling. Heart attacks hurt, don't they? This guy looks like he's having a sweet dream. That's far from normal, isn't it?"

M.E. Beckie O'Rourke shrugged. "Yeah, well, it's still a heart attack," she said evenly while wearing a look that said, "*Where'd you get* your *medical degree, asshole?*"

Burns crouched to get a closer look. The right fist was clenched. He pried it open and saw it held something. He took it and stood. "Know what this is?" he asked as he held it out for her to see.

"I dunno," said the M.E.

Burns called Officer Don into the room. "Know what this is?"

"Sure," came his reply, "It's a saxophone reed."

The detective looked down at the body. "I can't get over the look on his face. It's like just as he checked out, something, some... thought, gave him peace."

"Maybe so," said Officer Don, "But I would have been thinking: *I just died keeping a fifty-year-old, crappy mattress and box spring. Shit! Last thing I ever do and it's a fuck up!* So, I wouldn't be smiling."

"Well, this guy is," replied Burns.

Officer Don opened his mouth to speak, uttered a syllable, then stopped himself. Burns looked at him and turned up his hands. "What? What were you going to say, Sir Talks-a-lot?"

The officer, with a sheepish look, began, "Well, I was just remembering something my grandmother used to say. She said that when a person dies with a smile on their face, it's because they glimpsed their *first heaven* just as they passed."

"First heaven?" blurted the bemused detective.

"Yeah. She was very religious but had lots of crazy ideas of her own to go with it. She would say that when you leave this world, all your important wishes are fulfilled. Things that you always wanted, always dreamed of, would come to be. That heaven is a place where dreams come true."

"She also said that as you crossed over, you could have one foot in each world for a time. See or hear the world you're leaving behind just as the next world; your *first heaven* is being revealed. Like a parallel universe, ya know, that quantum stuff where everything is happening at once, the present, past, future."

Burns, thinking, *sorry I asked,* sighed, looked down at the deceased and said, "Hear that, pal? Looks like you got your wish!"

"Hey, who knows, there are crazier ideas," the officer said with a shrug.

"You'd be hard pressed to find one, pal."

The detective surveyed the space. Furniture and labeled boxes, stacked neatly, lined the walls. One box was open. It looked as though the deceased had been rooting through it. It was labeled *Jiggs.*

Peering into the open box, Burns mumbled, "I wonder who Jiggs is."

"You trying to be here all day?" asked the M.E.

"You're right," said the detective, "Tag him and bag him. I'm going home. The in-laws are coming for dinner."

"Nice, said the M.E., "What's LeVonne serving?"

Wincing, Burns replied, "Turkey."

## ACKNOWLEDGEMENTS

The unwavering support of my daughters, my grandsons, sister, cousins, and friends...

The push from my sweet Eileen to finally get this thing published...

The critiques and encouragement from the West Philly Writers group...

The invaluable production assistance from Ali Mogar, Jessica Prejean, Aaron Rosenberg, Julia Press Simmons, and Don Philbrick...

Remove one piece above and this book is just a Word doc on a laptop.

Thank you. Love you all.

—D

## ABOUT THE AUTHOR

Dennis Capoferri is a retired painting contractor. Currently writing his memoirs, he and his girlfriend Eileen share their time between an apartment in Philadelphia, PA and a house in Cape May Beach, NJ.

*Jiggs* is his first published work.

Made in the USA
Middletown, DE
14 October 2022

12674112R00106